Stranger in the Night

Suddenly the bat fluttered its wings extra fast. Everything went kind of hazy. I felt dizzy. I don't know what happened next exactly. I only remember that I heard a sound like a cork popping out of a champagne bottle.

When I could focus again, a tall, pale man was standing beside my bed. A thin mist swirled around his feet. A long black cape hung from his shoulders, and his jet black hair was slicked back from his pale face. "Good evening," he said, raising one elegant black eyebrow. "You are Michael McGraw, are you not?"

I nodded, wondering when he was going to bite my neck.

"Don't vorry—I am not going to bite your neck," he said as if he had read my mind. He had a deep voice and a funny accent that put the stress on the wrong syllable half the time. "I am here to enter your contest. . . ."

Monster of the Year

by
Bruce Coville

Illustrated by
Harvey Kurtzman

A GLC Book

A
MINSTREL®
BOOK

PUBLISHED BY POCKET BOOKS

New York   London   Toronto   Sydney   Tokyo

For Troy

This book is a work of fiction. Names, characters, places and incidents are either the product of the author's imagination or are used fictiously. Any resemblance to actual events or locales or persons, living or dead, is entirely coincidental.

A MINSTREL PAPERBACK *ORIGINAL*

 A Minstrel Book published by
POCKET BOOKS, a division of Simon & Schuster Inc.
1230 Avenue of the Americas, New York, NY 10020

Special thanks to Rich Hubeny of Penn Advertising for allowing me to visit his shop and for sharing his expertise in outdoor advertising, and to Pat MacDonald for her generous support.

Cover painting by Steve Fastner
Book Design by Alex Jay/Studio J
Typesetting by Jackson Typesetting
Editor: Tisha Hamilton

ISBN: 0-671-64749-0

First Minstrel Books Printing October 1989

10 9 8 7 6 5 4 3 2 1

A MINSTREL BOOK and colophon are registered trademarks of Simon & Schuster Inc.

Printed in the U.S.A.

Table of Contents

Chapter One

My Slightly Strange Family

THUD! That was me, falling off the couch.

"Something wrong, Mike?" asked my mother, without moving her eyes from her laptop computer.

I moaned softly. That got her to look up, so I crossed my eyes and let my tongue hang out.

Mom sighed. She knew what was coming, but now that I had her attention, she figured she had to ask anyway.

"What is it, Michael?"

"I'm bored. If I don't find something to do I'll die."

"So, go clean your room. Or are the junk-piles too high for you to get through the door?"

"Very funny," I said. "I mean it, Mom. Syracuse dies in August. I haven't been able to play baseball for a week because of the rain. I've read so many comic books my eyes are crossing. I'm going out of my mind!"

"The boy needs a job, Elsa," said a third voice. The words drifted out of a heat register at the base of the wall. "I say put him to work. Then the two of us can take a vacation."

My mother pushed aside her computer and went to kneel by the register. "Jeff, either come down and join us or stop eavesdropping."

"I wasn't eavesdropping," said my stepfather as he stepped through the living room door.

Mom glanced at the register, then back at my stepfather. "I thought you were upstairs, tearing out a wall."

"I was," said Jeff. "But I got tired." Curling his fingers, he used them to comb some flakes of plaster out of his brown beard. I could tell from his smirk that he had tiptoed down the stairs as fast as he could after he first spoke into the register. He loves doing that kind of thing, which should tell you a lot about him. "Besides," he continued, "this conversation sounded interesting."

"Well I'm glad *someone* has found *something* interesting around here," I said from the floor. "I'd feel bad if you were both as bored as I am."

"Boredom is a sign of mental deficiency," replied Jeff, wiping the plaster dust from his bald head. "The solution to this pathetic condition is to learn something. For example, you could learn about your mother's business."

"Thanks a lot, motor-mouth," said Mom.

"I'm serious," said Jeff. He stepped over me to sit on the couch. "It would be good for him. Better than lying here like a footstool," he added, placing his feet on my chest.

I shoved aside Jeff's boots and scrambled to my feet. "What a great idea!" I said. I love my mother's office—mostly because the people she hires are all a little strange.

"It would be a bad idea for Mike to hang around the house the rest of the summer," continued Jeff. "Just because I work at home doesn't mean I can keep an eye on him all the time. He could get in all kinds of trouble while I'm wrapped up in a story idea."

Jeff is a science-fiction writer. He's also kind of weird. (I think the two things probably go together.) But I like him a lot. In fact, when he adopted me I had my last name changed to McGraw, to match his. He meant more to me than a father I hadn't seen since I was six months old.

The funny thing is, my mother didn't change *her* name when they got married. She said she had changed it the first time she got married, and changed it back after the divorce, and that was enough. She planned to stay Elsa Adams for the rest of her life. This confuses outsiders, since they can't figure out who I really belong to, but it suits the three of us just fine.

What didn't suit Mom was the idea of me working for her. "Adams Billboard and Outdoor Advertising does not need a sixth grader hanging around the office all day," she said firmly.

"Adams B.O. Advertising needs all the help it can get," replied Jeff. "And what difference does sixth grade make? He starts seventh grade next month. And just last week you told me you needed a new gofer. So why not Mike?"

"If I'm going to be an animal, I'd rather be a gorilla."

"A gofer is an errand person," said Jeff. "Known as such because someone is always telling him to 'go fer' something. As, for example, right now I want you to 'go fer' a soda for me."

What Jeff really meant was "Get out of the room so I can work on your mother." So I headed for the kitchen.

I like our kitchen. It's a big old room with huge wooden cabinets and a blue tile floor. It may be kind of grungy, but it has "character," as my mother likes to say.

"Going downstairs for more soda!" I yelled, without checking the fridge. I figured that would give Jeff more time to convince Mom she should give me a job.

4

Our cellar is cool and deep and dark. But I never turn on the light before I start down the creaky wooden stairs. It's a little game I play— seeing how well I can get around down there in the dark. It's trickier than it sounds, because for some reason the previous owner put up rough wood walls that divide the cellar into sections.

Of course, it's usually not all that dark during the day. But on that particular afternoon the thunderclouds had darkened the sky and the cellar was too dim for me to see more than a few feet ahead of myself.

I moved slowly, groping my way along the rough wood of the cubicles. I was almost to the root cellar when a cold hand reached out of the darkness and grabbed the back of my neck.

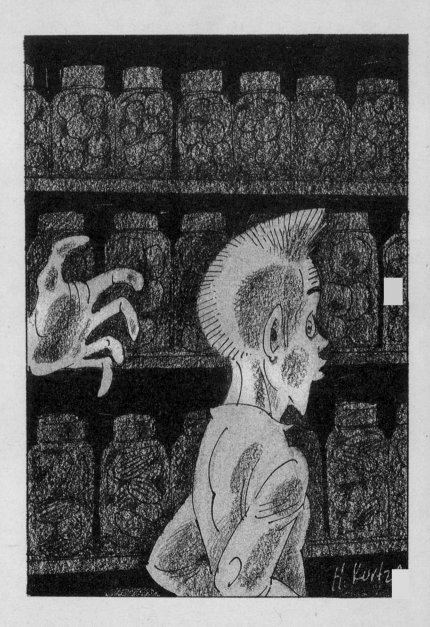

Chapter Two

Kevver

Kevver Smith was laughing so hard he could barely stand up. "You should see the look on your face!" he gasped, leaning against a post and pointing a small flashlight at me. "It's great."

I leaned against another post and glared at him. I wasn't mad at him for scaring me. After all, we've been playing "Gotcha!" for years now. I was mad because this put him several points ahead of me.

Kevver and I started sitting together in the cafeteria in first grade because we both had Frankenstein lunchboxes. When we discovered we were both born on the twenty-ninth of August that cemented things. We've been best friends ever since. We spend so much time together that we call each others' mother "Mom"—which gets us some funny looks when we're out in public, since Kevver is black and I'm white.

"How long have you been down here?" I asked.

"About three hours."

"Didn't you get bored?"

Kevver shrugged. "I brought some comics and my flashlight. Were you doing anything better than that?"

I shook my head. The rain was pounding against the tiny windows. Kevver followed me to the root cellar. We found a six-pack of cream soda, then clumped back up the stairs.

"Make a lot of noise," I said. "I want to make sure my folks know I'm coming."

"How come?"

I explained about the job idea, and how Jeff was trying to talk Mom into it.

"Man," said Kevver, "you are soooo lucky! That place is great. I wish I could work there."

"That's a good idea. If Mom says yes, let's see if we can get her to take you, too."

"Well, how did it go?" asked Jeff when we walked back into the living room. Kevver gave him the thumbs-up sign, and I realized that Jeff must have helped him hide in the cellar. The rat.

"So what about it?" I asked. "Do I get the job?"

My mother sighed. "We might as well give it a try," she said, reaching for a cream soda. She took a sip then leaned back against the couch and said, "I ought to have my head examined."

Jeff leaned over and stared into her hair. "It looks fine to me," he said. "In fact, I think it's quite lovely."

My mother snorted, and I decided to wait until supper to bring up the idea of having Kevver work at the shop. Her response was not encouraging. In fact, her exact words were, "You have got to be kidding!"

"I think it's a good plan," said Jeff, reaching for the mu shu pork.

We eat mu shu pork a lot. Mom claims she can run a business, make a house sparkle, and cook like Betty Crocker. She also says she has no interest in trying to do all three at the same time. So unless Jeff or I cook, which isn't very often, we eat take-out from the Chinese restaurant down the street. That's fine with me; I like the stuff.

"And just why is it a good plan?" asked my mother.

"Well, for one thing," said Jeff, scooping a pile of brown glop out of the carton, "young Kevver has excellent taste."

Mom rolled her eyes. "The fact that Kevver Smith thinks you're the world's greatest science-fiction writer does not mean I can use him at my office."

Jeff turned to pass me the carton. He gave me a

wink and said, "People who make billboards for a living need all the good taste they can get."

Mom started to growl, so I decided to wait until morning to bring the subject up again.

To my surprise, she brought it up first. "I thought about Kevver last night," she said, slathering cream cheese on her Sunday bagel. "Jeff is right. If the two of you are at the office and there's nothing to do, you can keep each other company—and stay out of my hair. But the first time I hear the words *I'm bored*, you're fired. Both of you!"

Jeff flashed me a grin. I decided to forgive him for letting Kevver in the cellar the day before.

Kevver stayed overnight. In the morning the three of us piled into Mom's car. I turned on the radio, so we could listen to our favorite DJ, "Skip" Toomaloo. He was singing one of his "morning songs."

> Oh, I know a girl, her name is Sue
> She's got lips like Superglue

My mother snapped off the radio, killing Skip's voice in mid-warble. "How can you listen to that moron?" she asked.

"Because he's more on than off," said Kevver.

I ignored the pun—Kevver makes them all the

time—and said to my mother, "Everybody listens to Skip. He's the most popular DJ in Syracuse."

"Well, I think he's disgusting," she said. "They never should have let him back on the air after that cat thing."

Everyone in Syracuse has an opinion on how station WERD should have handled the now infamous "Thirty Ways to Cook Your Cat" episode. Skip claimed he was just trying to find out if anyone else was really awake at five o'clock on Monday mornings. He said later that the way the studio switchboard lit up with protest calls showed the problem wasn't that people weren't awake, but that their sense of humor was still asleep.

After a flood of letters and newspaper editorials, the station banned Skip from the air for a week.

When he came back, his audience had tripled.

I was trying to decide what to say to my mother about all that when we pulled into the parking lot.

"Now remember," she said as we walked to the building, "this is an experiment. If it doesn't work out, I don't want any complaints. The first time—"

She didn't finish her sentence, because just then she tripped over a woman who was lying on the floor, moaning.

It was Wendy Moon, the company's billboard artist.

Wendy was young, and except for the fact that her nose pointed a little sideways, she was very pretty. She was dressed in black jeans and a black T-shirt. She had a black headband wrapped around her wispy blond hair, and a large piece of cardboard pinned to her chest. Written on it in huge, black letters were the words, *Art is Dead.*

Chapter Three

Wendy Moon

"Wendy, get up and stop blocking the doorway," snapped my mother. "And take off that ridiculous sign! I have some new employees I want you to meet and you're giving them a bad impression."

"A bad impression!" cried Wendy, climbing to her feet. "How can we give anyone a good impression, when we have clients like Ed the Plumber?" She darted behind the counter and held up a piece of stiff cardboard. A flap of tissue paper covered the front of it. "Have you seen this? Have you seen what this man wants to do to my design?"

We gathered around the drawing, which showed a man standing next to a maze of pipes. It was labeled, "Let the Amazing Mr. Ed Solve Your Plumbing Problems."

"Sounds like a laxative ad," said Kevver.

The drawing was very funny. I knew it was Wendy's work by the style. Unfortunately, the tissue paper overlay was filled with corrections and changes. The revised design was as dull as a pair of kindergarten scissors.

"It's pretty bad," agreed my mother. "On the other hand, it's Ed's billboard. If he wants a disaster, that's his choice."

"Agggh!" shrieked Wendy. She dropped her head against the counter. "Arrrgggh, aaaggggh, errrrgggh!"

She stood up, stomped into her office, and slammed the door. Two seconds later her hand reappeared to hang the Art is Dead sign on the doorknob.

"I knew this was going to be fun," whispered Kevver.

My mother sighed. "I do so love working with creative people," she said. "Well, I'll deal with Wendy later. Come on, boys. I'll show you where you're going to be stationed."

We followed her through a large double door into the shop, which is this huge area filled with the stuff they use to make billboards: metal panels for the painted boards, racks to hang them on, paint, brushes, the projector that blows up artwork to billboard size. Just tons of neat stuff.

Just inside of the doors to the right was a box as big as a room. Actually, it *was* a room. But in that huge space, it looked like a box. From other visits I knew this was a staff room. The shop crew gathered there in the morning for coffee, ate lunch there, and so on. Before Mom even opened the door I knew I would see a table, a coffee pot, and a wall covered with flyers, announcements, and small versions of her billboards.

What I didn't expect to see was the big man sitting at the table. He was wearing a grubby T-shirt. His muscular arms were about as thick as my legs. He had a gold tooth.

"Peter," said my mother, "I want you to meet our new gofers, Kevver and Michael."

The big man looked up and squinted at us. "Kids," he said, crushing his coffee cup. "I hate kids!" The cup was only cardboard, but the movement made Peter's bicep bulge like a softball.

"I take that back about this being fun," whispered Kevver.

But by late afternoon Kevver and I were feeling fairly comfortable with our job. The staff room had an intercom that people used to call us when they wanted something. We spent a lot of time delivering messages, sharpening pencils, and fetching fresh coffee.

The week went by in its own weird way. Wendy took to leaving little drawings for us to discover when we first arrived each day. Pete got friendly enough to growl hello each morning. We started to see how the business really worked.

Friday afternoon Kevver and I helped unload a shipment of paint. By the time we finished my arms were throbbing. "No wonder Pete looks the way he does," I whispered to Kevver.

He nodded. "If we keep this up, our muscles will be so big we can be superheroes for Halloween."

I smiled at the thought. Then I rubbed my aching shoulders. I wondered if it would be worth it.

We were heading back to the staff room when we heard a burst of angry voices explode from the front office. Without saying a word, we changed course and headed out the double doors.

It was Wendy again. At least, she was involved. But she wasn't making much noise this time. She was just standing in the corner, banging her head against the wall.

Chapter Four

Brainstorms

"I knew (*thump, thump*) this (*thump, thump*) was going to (*thump*) happen," moaned Wendy. "I just (*thump*) knew it."

"Now Wendy," said my mother, "settle down and get back over here. Let's see if we can work this out."

She was standing at the front counter, holding a billboard design. Next to her was a short, fierce-looking woman. She was dressed all in black, except for a large, round button that said, "BAM!" She looked familiar, though I couldn't figure out why.

Standing next to the woman in black was a man who could only be Ed the Plumber.

"That's amazing," whispered Kevver. "He looks just like the cartoon Wendy drew."

I nodded, but didn't say anything. I was trying to figure out what was going on.

"So you see, Mrs. Adams," said Ed, spreading his hands, "once Mrs. Smud talked to me, I decided not to go ahead with the billboard. I want to cancel."

"There *will* be a cancellation fee," said my mother sharply.

"No matter," snapped the woman in black. "BAM! will cover that cost."

She turned and stalked out of the office. Ed followed, looking sheepish. He paused at the door. "Do you think I should try television?" he asked. "I was talking to—"

"Out!" cried my mother. "Out, out, O-U-T OUT!"

Ed ducked through the door and disappeared.

"What was that all about?" I asked.

"Nothing much," she said softly. "Just Ed, coming to cancel his contract."

"Aaarrrghh!" cried Wendy, banging her head against the wall again.

"Didn't like the new design?" asked Kevver.

"He loved it," said my mother. "Only he's not going to do billboards anymore."

"Why not?"

Mom held up a button identical to the one Mrs. Smud had been wearing. "BAM! stands for 'Billboards Are Monstrous!' Myrna Smud wants to ban outdoor advertising, and she's starting with us because she thinks we make the most offensive billboards in town."

"What's wrong with them?" asked Kevver.

"According to Myrna, they're too imaginative. She says stimulating the imagination leads to crime."

"Sheesh!" said Kevver. "Next thing you know she'll want to ban fairy tales."

"She's working on it," said Mom grimly.

Suddenly I realized why Mrs. Smud had looked familiar to me. I had seen her hanging around our school last spring. "She's the one who was trying to ban all those books from our library!" I shouted.

I was really mad now. This woman wanted to shut down both my mother and my brain. I wanted to strike back. But it wasn't until the next morning that I figured out how to do it.

It was one of those ideas that grows slowly, then suddenly explodes. It started at breakfast. It was Saturday, and Kevver had stayed overnight. Jeff decided to make bacon and pancakes for breakfast. Mom joined us in the kitchen. When the four of us sat down to eat together we were still complaining about Myrna.

"Can we change the topic?" asked Jeff. "Talking about censorship while I eat gives me indigestion." He paused for a moment, then brightened.

"You guys have a birthday coming up. What do you want?"

"A billboard," I said, without even thinking about it.

"That's ridiculous," said my mother. "Do you know how much a billboard is worth?"

"No."

She told me. I almost choked on my pancake. But I didn't give up. "What's an empty billboard worth?" I asked.

"Nothing," she said. "It's just a drain on the company. When I think about what Ed did yesterday—" She stopped in the middle of her sentence, but it was too late.

I smiled sweetly. "Ed the Plumber's contract for that billboard was supposed to start on my birthday. Don't you see, Mother—this is fate! It's like it was planned. We can't resist it."

Kevver picked up the battle. "I think it's a neat idea. I'd like one, too."

"We could share!" I cried, trying to give my mother the idea that this would save money.

She looked at me with a puzzled expression. "What would you do with a billboard if you had one?"

"Let me think about it," I said.

Mom smirked, which I did not take to be a good sign.

After breakfast Kevver and I examined one of Mom's media kits. These are folders she uses to show clients the kinds of signs we make. I figured it might give us some ideas.

"How about a public service billboard?" asked Kevver. "This says the company donates a few billboards to good causes every year. If we can convince your Mom we're doing something worthwhile, she might say yes."

"Sounds pretty dull to me," I said.

"Wait!" cried Kevver. "I've got it! Let's tell her it will be educational."

I made a face. "That sounds even duller than a public service billboard."

"No, you don't understand. We tell her it's going to be educational for *us*. We'll do the look-how-much-we'll-learn-from-this number on her."

"I like it!" I said. "Do you think we'd be pressing it if I tell her I want to learn the family business?" I frowned. "Of course, if that old bat Myrna Smud has her way, there won't be a family business much longer."

That was when it hit me. I've heard about inspiration, but this was the first time I ever experienced it. I felt as if a bolt of lightning had just sizzled through my skull.

"Oh, wait!" I cried. "What if we use the billboard to take a shot at BAM? Mom ought to like

21

that. After all, Myrna and BAM! are the reason the billboard is empty anyway."

Kevver was immediately caught by the idea. Listen, BAM! stands for 'Billboards are Monstrous!' right? So why not make a *monster* billboard?"

It took another two days, and a lot of help from Jeff, but we finally wore my mother down.

"All right," she said. "You win. You can have the sign for one month. But here are the conditions."

And then she handed me a contract.

I couldn't believe it. A contract from my own mother!

"Hey," she said. "You want to get involved with the business? Then do it in a businesslike way."

The contract was pretty official looking; Mom had even written it on company paper. It had some gobbledygook in it, but most of the important parts were right to the point.

For this sign, Adams Billboard and Outdoor Advertising will provide:
* paint and other necessary supplies
* two days of staff time
* one month of display on the structure adjacent to Erie Boulevard and Tanner Avenue

Michael McGraw and Kevver Smith will provide:
* concept for the sign

* labor and talent necessary to finish the sign
Sign concept and design to be approved by Elsa
Adams before work commences.

"What does this mean?" I asked, pointing to
the part about what Kevver and I would supply.
"It means I expect you to do your share. Wendy
will help with the design, and Peter will set you up
for the painting. But I can only afford to give you
two days of their time. So be careful how you
use it."

"So what kind of sign do you guys want?"
asked Wendy, after my mother had explained to
her what was going on.
"Something with monsters," I replied.
Wendy pulled a BAM! button out of her cork-
board wall. "Billboards Are Monstrous," she said,
pointing to the letters. "You guys wouldn't be
trying to rattle Myrna Smud's cage, would you?"
Kevver and I smiled.
"That's cool," said Wendy. "This should be fun."
We started brainstorming. Let me tell you, thinking can be hard work. But it was fun, too. We
threw around a million stupid ideas, kept a few,
put parts of different ideas together. Wendy
sketched like mad all the time we were talking,
tossing sheet after sheet of paper into her waste-

23

basket. It took almost six hours, but we finally settled on a billboard announcing a Monster of the Year contest.

The design showed Frankenstein's monster, with Dracula and the Wolfman peering over his shoulders. All three were staring at the Bride of Frankenstein. Along the base of the drawing eerie black letters proclaimed, "ENTER THE MONSTER OF THE YEAR CONTEST TODAY!"

We thought it was pretty funny. How could we guess anyone would take it seriously?

Chapter Five

Sign Up

"Kids," snorted Pete when he saw our design the next morning.

Shaking his head, he stomped over to a stack of tall, thin metal panels standing against the wall. His muscles bulged as he lifted a panel and carried it over to the rack. Hoisting the panel a little higher, he set the hooks on the back over the rack's crossbars. *Snap!* The panel clicked into place. "No one told me I was going to have to work with kids," he muttered as he headed back to get the next panel.

"Ignore him," said Wendy. "He's terrified he might have a pleasant thought before he gets his listing for 'Longest Bad Mood in the History of the World' in the *Guinness Book of Records*."

Snap! Another panel clicked into place.

"Back soon," said Wendy and headed for the door.

"Hey, you two!" yelled Pete. "You're big enough to help with this. Grab a panel and start moving."

The panels were twelve feet high and just over two feet wide. When they were all in place we would paint our sign on them.

By working together, Kevver and I were able to slide a panel over the floor to the rack. With me standing at one edge and Kevver at the other, we managed to heave it off the floor. It took a couple of tries to catch the hooks onto the crossbars.

"Good,' said Pete, when he saw that we could do it. "I've got other work to do. You can finish this yourselves."

Wendy came back just as we were putting up the last panel. She was carrying the final artwork, which she had done with transparent inks on a sheet of clear plastic. She put the artwork on the tray of a projector. When she switched on the machine, a twelve-foot-high image of the Bride of Frankenstein appeared on the panels.

"All right!" I cried.

"Your mom told me to remind you that you've only got six hours of my time left," said Wendy, as she opened a can of paint. "So pay attention while I show you what to do. You'll have to do most of this on your own."

Three days, seven paint spills, and one near fall

from a ladder later, our sign was ready to face the world.

On the morning of the big day, Pete and his crew took apart the metal panels and loaded them onto one of the company lift trucks. Kevver and I followed in a pick-up truck, with Wendy driving. It took about twenty minutes to get to the "structure," which is what you call the frame that holds a billboard.

Pete handed me a pair of work gloves. "Climb in," he said, pointing to a big metal bucket on the back of the lift truck. "We're going up."

I did as he told me. Pete got in beside me. Then somebody flipped a switch, and the bucket started going up. I wasn't about to let Pete see how nervous I was, so I gripped the edge of the bucket and smiled as we floated into the air. I guess maybe it showed anyway, because when I got back to earth Kevver told me I was as green as the monster on the billboard.

My mother showed up just as we were maneuvering the last two strips of metal into place. "Not bad, boys," she said after staring at the sign for a while.

"Not bad?" cried Kevver. "It's gorgeous!"

I agreed. Twelve feet high, forty-eight feet long, and all monster, our sign was the most beautiful thing I had ever seen.

Even so, I wasn't prepared for what happened when we started driving home that night. Mom had the radio on to get the report from the traffic helicopter. Most of it sounded like it does every night. The big difference was the last bit, when the pilot said, "The only unexpected problem is the big curve on the boulevard. Westbound traffic there is running a little slow because people are still gawking at that new billboard—the one with all the monsters."

I looked at Kevver. He looked at me. My mother made a funny sound. "I can't believe it," she said. "I just can't believe it."

"Oh, come on, Mom," said Kevver. "If you really believe in your business, it shouldn't surprise you when people pay attention to a billboard."

"It doesn't surprise me," she said. "It annoys me. I've been trying to get that kind of reaction to a billboard for twenty years!"

The next morning it seemed like every radio station in town was talking about the sign. We even got mentioned on the Skip Toomaloo show, which Mom let us listen to for a change.

As it turned out, part of what made the sign so fascinating was that no one could figure out what we were trying to sell. (No one even guessed that we weren't trying to sell anything; that was too unbelievable for words.) Most people figured it was a stunt to drum up interest in some new product or film that would be announced in the fall. But they were dying to know what it was— partly because they loved our sign so much.

We knew they loved it because when one of the local TV stations covered the story (another shock for my mother) the people they talked to were all laughing and smiling; well, all except one. The last interview was with Myrna Smud, and when she talked about the sign she looked like she had just been chewing on a lemon.

"This monster mania is terrible for our children," she fumed. "It stimulates their imagination, excites their minds. It could give them . . . *ideas*!"

"Now there's a terrible thought," said Jeff when he heard Myrna on the news. "Children getting ideas. Another sign of the decline of western civilization."

We hadn't set out to keep the sign's origin a secret, so any good reporter could have followed our trail. Several did, and three days after the sign went up Kevver and I had our pictures on the front page of the morning paper. That was exciting in itself. But what came next was even more thrilling.

We were sitting in the staff room, waiting for someone to ask us to do an errand when it happened. Mom's secretary buzzed us on the intercom. "Phone call for you boys," she said.

"Both of us?" I asked.

"That's what the man said."

We headed for the front desk. When I took the phone a familiar voice said, "Michael McGraw? I want you and your friend to be on my show tomorrow morning." I almost fell over. It was Skip Toomaloo! We were going to be ON the Skip Toomaloo Show.

To celebrate, Kevver and I got Jeff to drive us out to the billboard that night. It seemed especially appropriate to go in his car because he drives an old hearse—a funeral car. Jeff loves that car; he says its part of his image. Mom doesn't like it so much. She says if he considers it part of his image he must use a fun-house mirror when he shaves.

Anyway, we piled into the hearse and Jeff took us for ice cream, then drove us over to admire our billboard.

The sun was setting behind it when we arrived. I sat there, licking my butter brickle ice cream and admiring our beautiful monsters. As the light faded, I thought I saw something begin flapping around the sign. Then I saw another, and another. Before I knew it there were dozens.

"What kind of birds are those?" I asked, motioning with my ice cream cone.

Jeff squinted at the sign. "Those aren't birds."

"Well what are they?" asked Kevver.

Jeff hesitated. He looked at the sign, and then at us. "They're bats," he said at last.

I felt myself shiver—and it wasn't from the ice cream.

And still the bats kept coming—more and more, until there were thousands of them flying around the sign. The sound of their wings was like distant thunder. Suddenly, as if they had heard some kind of signal, they all flew away at once. All except one.

The last bat fluttered over to the hearse. It circled us three or four times, flapping at the windows, before it flew off to join the others.

Chapter Six

Telegram from Transylvania

Skip was on the air when we arrived at the radio station the next morning. I could see him through the glass wall of the booth. He was tall and slender, with a long, pointy moustache. While we were waiting for him, someone came up behind us and said, "Are you the guys that made the sign?"

We turned around and found ourselves facing a *very* pudgy girl.

"Well, are you?" she demanded.

I nodded, wondering what this kid was doing here.

"That's neat," she said. "I love monsters. Mostly because I am one."

"That's nice," I said. I glanced back through the window. I hoped Skip would come out soon. I didn't want to have to listen to this kid much longer.

"So, you like my father's show?"

I looked at her. "Your father?" I asked.

Just then the door to the soundbooth opened and Skip skipped out. (I mean it!) "Hello, boys," he said cheerfully, reaching out to shake our hands. "I see you've already met my daughter, Lulu."

As I shook his hand I was thinking, *What kind of a man would name his own daughter Lulu Toomaloo?*

But Skip seemed nice enough. He bought us a couple of sodas and told us what to expect when we went on the air.

"There's nothing to be nervous about," he said several times. "Pretend we're having a conversation in your living room. I'll just ask you about the billboard—how you got the idea, that kind of thing." He glanced at his watch. "News break is nearly over," he said. "Come on—let's go."

We followed him into the sound booth. He sat down, slipped on his earphones, and took a sip of coffee.

Instantly, a horrible look crossed his face. He spit the coffee back into his cup. Covering the microphone, he turned to his daughter and said, "Lulu, did you do this?"

Lulu Toomaloo returned her father's look with wide, innocent eyes. I'm not a kid for nothing. I could tell everything that was going on between them. Of course she had done it. He knew that. She knew that he knew. And he knew that she knew that he knew.

But admitting any of that would spoil the fun. So Lulu placed a pudgy hand against her face and let a single tear spill out of her right eye. It rolled slowly down her round, red cheek. "I guess maybe I did, Daddy Dear," she simpered.

I thought I was going to throw up. I don't think Skip took it much better, because I noticed that his right eye started to twitch. He began fiddling with the ends of his moustache.

"Now, Lulu," he said, "you know it's not nice to put salt in Daddy's coffee. It makes Daddy very unhappy."

Lulu smiled up at him, which almost caused her blue eyes to disappear behind her fat cheeks. "But, Daddy," she said, "I love to see the funny face you make. That face makes Lulu happy!"

We learned later that Lulu put something in her father's coffee once a week. To make things worse, she always did it at different times. This meant that Skip never knew *when* it was going to happen—or *what* it was going to be. In the past six months Lulu had spiced his coffee with vanilla, hair oil, and tabasco sauce. But those were for variety. Usually it was just salt, which worked well for Lulu's purposes, since it dissolved quickly and didn't smell.

What made all this especially cruel was that Skip really loved his coffee. As a morning DJ, it was the fuel that made his life possible. But the first sip of each new cup had become an adventure in anticipation. When would Lulu strike next?

Actually, from what Skip told Kevver later, that was only one of the questions that burned in his brain. The others included: Where did this kid come from? Is she really mine? Why is she doing this to me?

The answers to those questions were all very simple. Lulu had come from the same place all babies come from. She was indeed his. And she was doing this because she had a permanent, unending grudge against her parents for naming her Lulu Toomaloo. While some kids might have learned to laugh off the name, Lulu figured she had been permanently wronged. She had every intention of making her parents pay for what they had done.

Of course, things might not have been so bad if Lulu's parents hadn't spoiled her rotten before she ever understood how remarkably silly her name was. But as a baby, whatever Lulu wanted, Lulu got. I guess her parents figured it was better than hearing her scream.

Unfortunately for Lulu, most of what she wanted was edible, which was why she looked like she was in training as a replacement for the Goodyear Blimp.

But those were all things that we learned later. The only thing we learned about her that day at the station was that she was the most spoiled kid we had ever seen.

So who would have guessed that she would have been part of the great thing that happened next?

I first found out about it a few mornings later, when my mother called me and Kevver into her office. She had a funny look on her face—kind of like she had just seen a flying saucer or something.

"You OK, Mom?" I asked.

She nodded.

"What's going on?" asked Kevver

"Station WERD just called. They want to sponsor the contest."

"What contest?" I asked, ignoring the obvious answer. It was so ridiculous it never even crossed my mind.

"The Monster of the Year Contest," she said. "I told them I was going to take down the billboard in three weeks, and they said they'd pay to keep it up." She shook her head as thought she was in a daze. "They plan to buy space on other

37

structures, too. They want to build their whole fall promotion around your idea."

Kevver and I let out a whoop.

We were interrupted by Mom's secretary. "Telegram, Ms. Adams," she said from the doorway.

Mom looked startled. She took the yellow envelope and opened it. She grinned. "Listen to this. 'Monster of the Year Contest is great idea. Stop. Will be in touch. Stop. The Count.' "

"How could someone know about the contest already?" I asked.

"Oh, I'm sure it's from the station," said Mom. "Just a way of saying, 'Welcome aboard.' "

But I thought about the bats we had seen flying around the billboard, and I wasn't so sure. What I was thinking seemed too silly to say out loud, so I kept it to myself. But I was beginning to get a little nervous.

Over the next few weeks the Monster of the Year Contest took on a life of its own. Once my mother got over her shock she started to work out ways to take advantage of the situation.

She also gave me and Kevver a bonus. She said letting us have a billboard was the best investment she'd ever made. I realized then that it might be possible to make money doing something I liked.

Jeff felt pretty smug about the whole thing. I

could tell he was having trouble not teasing my mother about what a good idea it had been to hire us—especially when the story was picked up by the international wire services.

The first entries came from local people. Some announced the monsters they would be impersonating. Others began to stretch the term. A teacher entered one of her former students. Secretaries sent in entries for their bosses. People began talking about entering the mayor.

Kevver and I had fun going through the entry forms, even if we did have to put up with Lulu while we did it.

Then we got another telegram. It was from Transylvania.

Greetings. Stop. Will arrive Syracuse in two days. Stop. Bringing entrant for M.O.T.Y. contest. Stop. Please arrange accommodations. Stop. Igor.

Chapter Seven

Waiting for Igor

"Is this a gag?" I asked.

"It must be," said Kevver. "Transylvania is a made-up place."

"Not so," said Jeff. He ran a hand over his shiny head. "Transylvania was absorbed into Rumania decades ago, so people don't talk about it much anymore. But it's a real place."

He reached for the telegram. "We might find out something about this by calling Western Union. I'm guessing it's just a joke. You should consider it a compliment. Someone else is playing the kind of reality game you two started when you put up a sign for a contest that didn't exist."

"But now it does exist," I said.

Jeff looked at me. "What are you saying?" he asked.

I stopped. What was I saying? That what we did changed the way things really were? That seemed

40

silly. I shrugged. "I don't know," I said. "Just talking, I guess."

"Well, stop talking and come eat," yelled my mother from the kitchen. "I don't plan to cook supper again for at least a month, so I want you to pay proper attention to this one."

My mother's claim that she can cook like Betty Crocker isn't far off. If she wasn't running a business, and my stepfather wasn't a truly weird science fiction writer, we could have a normal home, like on "Leave It to Beaver."

I mentioned that to Jeff once. He just looked at me and said, "If pigs had wings, they could fly." I wasn't exactly sure what he meant by that, but it didn't matter. I wasn't complaining. I pretty much like things the way they are.

When I went to bed that night I took the telegram up to my room and hung it over my desk. It was cool having a telegram from Transylvania.

But it got a little spooky when the second one arrived.

Greetings. Stop. Arriving at airport 9:30 PM, EST, October 15. Stop. Please secure accommodations and arrange to meet us. Stop. Igor.

We were at the radio station, sorting through

the mail that had come in about the contest. We could have sorted through it at home, of course, but Lulu always wanted to be involved. Since it turned out that one reason the station had decided to support the contest was that she had offered her father various threats about what would happen if they didn't, we could hardly refuse to let her help. But we weren't happy about it.

I suppose we sound kind of stuck-up. But you know how it is—little kids always want to hang around with big kids, and big kids always want little kids to leave them alone. That's just the way it is. We didn't hold the fact that Lulu was a girl against her that much. What we had against her—besides her being a little kid—was that she was obnoxious. I mean, would you want to be friends with a kid whose idea of fun was pushing up the end of her nose and making piggy noises at you? A kid who thought dropping ice cubes down your back was a sign of affection? A kid who liked to stuff a whole candy bar in her mouth, chew it for thirty seconds, and then stick out her tongue?

The more I saw of Lulu, the sorrier I felt for Skip. That bothered me. Skip had been a kind of hero for me. But it's hard to look up to someone you feel sorry for.

Anyway, we did most of our work on the contest at the station after school. Jeff drove us in twice a week to look at entries and discuss details for the big night.

Halloween was on a Monday. The plan was for the station to throw a huge party the Friday before that. Anyone who wanted to take part had to show up in costume or display whatever it was that made them monstrous. People who had nominated their boss or some local politician would be allowed to explain why they thought their candidate should win—though we didn't figure too many folks would try that. "Good way to get fired" was the way Jeff put it.

Then Kevver and I would do the judging, and give out the trophy.

We had billboards all over the city now. And every kid in school was talking about the contest. (And were they ever jealous of Kevver and me.) So things were rolling along pretty well.

At least until the fifteenth of October.

Jeff decided we should go to the airport, just in case someone named Igor really did show up. Mom wouldn't come—she thought we were just being silly. Lulu, on the other hand, insisted on going.

We drove over in Jeff's hearse, which seemed appropriate. Because it had only one seat, Kevver and I got to ride in back, far away from Lulu. Of course Jeff had to put up with her, but we figured it wouldn't hurt him. Besides, he could always use her in his next book.

The airport was nearly deserted when we arrived, which wasn't surprising. Not many flights come into Syracuse on Saturday evening.

We checked the big flight board. The only thing coming in at nine-thirty was a Baltic Air Transport flight. But it was listed as coming from New York City.

"Well, no flights from Transylvania," I joked, feeling a little nervous.

Jeff shrugged. "You wouldn't expect a direct flight here from Rumania. Anyone flying in would probably have to make several stopovers."

He talked as if he actually expected someone to show up. Maybe he did. We had discussed the telegram over and over, again, and our current theory was that if it wasn't a joke, it was from a film company trying for free publicity. That was OK with us. It would make the contest all that much more fun.

We decided to go to the indoor observation deck to wait for the plane. A large glass wall looked out over the airfield. The night was dark and moonless—soon it started to rain. A flash of lightning streaked through the sky. Thunder rumbled.

"Baltic Air Transport flight number one has been delayed," announced the loudspeaker. "Arrival is now anticipated at ten o'clock."

Half an hour later the flight was delayed again. I wasn't surprised. The weather was really awful.

Jeff glanced at his watch. "I hope we're not waiting here for nothing," he said.

"I'm bored," whined Lulu. She had been saying that off and on after the first five minutes. Jeff gave her some money and told her to go get herself a snack.

No wonder she was so fat. I bet people gave her money and told her to go get food a lot.

Time dragged, and I fell asleep for a while. I'm not sure why we didn't just go home. I suppose it was because we had spent so much time there already. You know how it is—you start something, and then decide you're going to finish it, No Matter What.

Finally I heard the announcement: "Baltic Air Transport flight number one will land in exactly five minutes."

I looked at the clock.

It was five minutes to midnight.

Chapter Eight

The Mysterious Crate

At midnight the biggest bolt of lightning I had ever seen split the sky.

Then the rain stopped—just stopped, as if someone had turned off a faucet. Puddles gleamed on the runways as a plane came in for a landing. The four of us stood with our faces pressed against the glass of the observation window, staring at it. All was silent, until Lulu found that she could make rude noises by blowing on the glass.

A shiver whispered down my spine when the plane landed. It was small and black, with wings shaped like a bat's.

Jeff laughed. "That settles it. It has to be a film company. Come on, kids. This should be fun."

"Wait a second," said Kevver. "Let's watch."

Even after the passengers got off the plane we would have plenty of time to get to the meeting area. So we decided to wait.

Soon two men wheeled a ramp up to the plane. The door opened and we waited for the passengers.

There was only one—a short, hump-backed man, wearing a white lab coat.

I shivered again, and we headed for the escalator. We were waiting when the man came shuffling through the gate—Kevver and I close together, Lulu behind us. I don't think she was scared. She just liked to check out a situation before she made up her mind what kind of damage she was going to cause.

"Igor"—or whoever he was—came shuffling down the corridor, dragging one foot behind him. He had long, dark hair. One eye was half-closed in a kind of squint. One arm swung freely, and he kept the other tight against him.

Jeff stepped forward to greet him. "Igor, I presume?" he said with a smile on his face.

Remembering the movie *Young Frankenstein*, I almost expected him to say, "It's *Eye*-gore." But he didn't. Neither did he take Jeff's hand. Instead he grabbed Jeff's arm. "We have no time to lose!" he said desperately. "We must get to the baggage claim."

When no one moved right away he said, "Is there something wrong with you? Hurry!"

Kevver swung into action. "It's this way," he said. He started down the hall. The rest of us trailed after him.

47

Igor clumped along beside me. "Let's hope the tranquilizer doesn't wear off before we get there," he said. Then he gave me the weirdest smile I had ever seen.

"I'm hungry," said Lulu. We ignored her.

The baggage claim area was empty.

"Good," said Igor. "We're in time." He sounded almost disappointed.

The luggage carriers were moving. After a few moments several large black bags came sliding out from behind the wall.

"Grab them!" cried Igor. He lurched forward and snatched the first two off the conveyor belt himself. I dived for the next one. Kevver got the two after that.

"Well, here I am, stuck with a couple of old bags," he said.

"Don't mind him," Jeff told Igor. "He has an uncontrollable urge to make bad puns. Aside from that, he's a good kid."

"Remarks about kids really get my goat!" said Kevver happily. I could see he was just getting started. But before he could come up with another groaner a door at the side of the baggage area opened. A man came through, pushing a hand cart ahead of him. On the cart was a huge wooden crate. It was covered with red signs that said, "FRAGILE! HANDLE WITH CARE!"

"Package for a Mr. Eye-gore!" yelled the man.

"That's Ee-gore!" we all yelled. The man shrugged. Something thumped inside the crate.

"Quick," cried Igor, "help him get it off the cart." He thumped over to the man. Jeff joined him. Kevver and I put down the bags we were holding and ran over, too.

"I'm hungry," said Lulu.

The crate was at least eight feet tall. And was it ever heavy! But between the five of us we managed to wrestle it to the floor. As we did, I heard something start thumping inside of it.

"We're too late!" yelled Igor. "Stand back."

Before I could move, a huge green fist smashed up through the boards. Splinters flew in all directions.

The man who had brought the crate screamed and ran back through the doors.

A rumbling roar came from inside the crate as another fist smashed up through the wood.

"This is great!" cried Jeff.

I wasn't so sure I agreed.

"Reeooarrrr!"

The hands disappeared. I heard a horrible creaking noise—as if nails were being ripped out of wood. They were. The lid of the crate started to lift into the air.

Igor spun around and snatched one of the black

bags. "Don't let him out!" he cried, rummaging through the bag. "Don't let him out!"

Kevver and I looked at each other, uncertain of what to do. While we dithered, Lulu went and sat on the top of the crate.

"Reeaaooorrr!" rumbled the deep voice.

"Calm down!" snapped Igor. He scurried back to the crate, carrying a hypodermic needle in his right hand.

"What's that?" asked Jeff.

"Elephant tranquilizer. Now, if the young lady would kindly move."

"I'm hungry," said Lulu, getting off the end of the crate.

Immediately the lid wrenched away from the rest of the box. Igor jabbed forward with the needle. An outraged cry rang through the empty baggage area. It echoed for a time, fading finally to an eerie silence.

With a thump, the lid fell back into place.

Chapter Nine

Guess Who's Coming to Breakfast?

"You may take us to our hotel now," said Igor.

"Aren't you going to let your friend out?" asked Jeff.

Igor shook his head. "Flying makes him airsick. He will not calm down for another day or so. Until then—well, it is best that he stay where he is."

He took a hammer from one of his bags and started to pound the nails back into the crate. Of course, that still left two big holes in the top. I was dying to peek through one of them to see what was inside. But I had a terrible vision of those hands thrusting out again. If that happened I could get the biggest black eye in the history of the world. Either that, or lose my head altogether.

"I have to get the car," said Jeff. "Kids, why don't you come with me?"

We followed him down the hall. When I looked

back, Igor was sitting on the crate, pounding one last nail back into place.

"Well, what do you think?" asked Jeff when we were far enough away that Igor couldn't hear us.

"I think I'm hungry," said Lulu.

"I think they're great," said Kevver. "Or at least, Igor is. Who knows if there's anyone in the box or not?"

I started to ask what he meant, then figured it out for myself. All it would take for someone to create the effect we had just seen would be a sound box, a remote control and a couple of mechanical arms.

"That Igor guy must really want to win the contest," I said. I wasn't about to admit that I thought Igor and the box were for real. It made me feel pretty silly.

Lulu didn't worry about feeling silly. "I think they're real," she said. "By the way, I'm still hungry."

We happened to be passing a candy machine, so we took up a collection. Between Jeff, Kevver, and me we had enough change to get something for Lulu to stuff into her mouth.

She was happy. But I wasn't, not until I had an explanation that made sense of all this. "Why would anyone want to win the contest this much?" I asked.

"I can think of half a dozen reasons," said Jeff. He started to tick them off on his fingers. "One: it's someone who (a) has money and (b) loves monsters—sort of how you and Kevver might turn out if you ever get rich. Two: some film company is taking advantage of your contest to get some extra publicity. Fair enough. This whole thing is about publicity. Three: some company is going to use the contest to introduce a new product. You know, one of those monstery breakfast cereals or something. Four: some nut has decided—"

"OK, OK," I said, holding up my hands to stop him. "You've convinced me."

"Good," said Jeff. "Because I'd hate to have you think those guys are for real. This *is* just a joke."

I didn't know if he was trying to convince me, or himself.

I tried another question. "If they're fakes, why did you ask Igor if he was going to let his friend out of the box?"

"I was just playing the game," said Jeff. He took out his keys and unlocked the hearse. "Good thing we decided to bring this baby," he said as we climbed into the long, black car. "Otherwise Igor would have needed to rent a van to get that crate of his to the hotel."

54

"Mom will be amazed that this thing actually turned out to be useful," said Kevver. He knew how my mother felt about the hearse.

Igor was waiting for us at the front of the airport. With a lot of dragging and thumping, we managed to get the crate into the back of the hearse. It slid into the spot where coffins used to ride as if it had been made for it.

"My wife made reservations for you at the Karloff Hotel," said Jeff when Igor climbed into the front seat. "I hope that will be satisfactory."

"We shall see," said Igor. He slammed the door and we drove away with Lulu, Kevver, and me keeping the crate company in the back.

"I'm hungry," said Lulu. She crossed her eyes, pushed up the end of her nose, and started to make snorting noises.

The rain started again. Jagged bolts of lightning flashed all around us. The thunder sounded like exploding bombs. And then the thing in the crate began to moan.

It was still pouring when we pulled up in front of the hotel. "You kids wait here," said Jeff before he and Igor climbed out of the hearse.

I glanced down at the moaning crate. Jeff read the look on my face. "Don't be silly," he said. He hesitated, then added, "Look, if you have any problems, come and get me."

Then he slipped out of the car and disappeared into the rain.

We waited. Five minutes went by, and then ten. Other than a few thumps and moans, the box was quiet. I pressed my face against the cold glass of the passenger window to see if I could spot Jeff. Lightning sizzled down to my right through the thick rain. The clap of thunder that followed made me jump. It seemed to scare whatever was in the box, too. It thumped the sides and began to moan louder.

"I'm hungry," said Lulu nervously. "I think I'll go inside to get some food."

"I could use a candy bar myself," said Kevver. "Besides, this is the wrong time of the day for 'Good Moaning.' "

I didn't bother to groan at the pun. The box was doing enough groaning for all of us.

I opened the back door and we stepped into the rain. Drops the size of quarters spattered against us. We were soaked before we'd gone five feet from the hearse.

We bolted through the revolving door and into the hotel. I was peeling my soaked shirt away from my skin when I heard Igor shout, "This is an outrage!"

I turned and saw him banging his fist against the desk. Then he climbed on a chair, so that he could look the desk clerk in the eye. "It's an outrage!" he cried again.

"I'm sorry, sir," said the clerk. He looked pretty frightened. "But there is nothing I can do about it. Perhaps if you come back tomorrow?"

Jeff sighed. "Come on," he said to Igor. "We won't get anywhere with this guy. I'll take you to our place for the night. Maybe we can work this out in the morning."

Our place? Jeff was going to bring this nut home? I shook my head and reminded myself that it was all just some kind of stunt.

But if this guy was here from some movie company, what was the problem? Why wouldn't the hotel let him in?

"They won't accept his money," explained Jeff as we drove off through the pelting rain.

"An outrage!" muttered Igor. "An offense to my homeland. "I shall report them to the embassy!" He paused. "Better yet, I shall have a press conference!"

Well, there it was—a press conference. Must be Jeff was right after all. This was just a publicity stunt.

We dropped Lulu off at her place. Her parents were waiting up for her. As she ran to the door I heard her shout, "I'm home! What's to eat?"

We waited until Lulu was inside before driving away.

"A most strange little girl," said Igor, nodding back at the Toomaloo house.

He was the first person I had ever met who seemed too weird to call Lulu strange.

Mom was asleep when we got home. We had called her several times from the airport, so she knew about all the delays. About the fourth call she said she was going to bed, and we could tell her all about it in the morning.

Boy, was she in for a surprise.

"Do you think the crate will be all right out here for the night?" asked Jeff when we pulled into the driveway.

Igor looked as though we had just suggested that we sell one of his children. "Are *you* trying to insult us, too?" he asked.

"Of course not," said Jeff hastily. "I just thought—"

"We take him inside with us," said Igor. "Or else I stay out here—a fact I shall mention in my press conference tomorrow."

"Hey, it's OK," said Jeff. "We'll take it—him—inside."

Inside wasn't good enough. Igor insisted that the crate had to go up to the spare room with him. So we started dragging it up the stairs. The noise woke my mother. When she came into the hall to see what was going on, she just shook her head and said, "I can't believe I married that man."

Without another word, she turned and went back to bed.

Igor was incredibly strong, so it wasn't as hard as I had thought it would be to get the crate upstairs. Even so, by the time we had both Igor and the crate settled, Kevver and I were so exhausted we could hardly see straight.

"Good night, boys," said Igor as he closed the door to his room. "Sleep well. And don't be afraid. Nothing is going to happen—*tonight*." Then he gave us a weird laugh and closed his door.

"That guy is major strange," said Kevver.

I nodded. But I was too tired to think about it right then. I don't even remember getting into bed. I just know sleep felt awfully good.

When I woke up, I wondered if the whole thing had been a dream. Kevver said if it was, we had been having the same dream.

We went downstairs for our usual Sunday morning breakfast. "Morning, Mom!" I said. I was trying to be cheerful, so I was kind of insulted when she started to scream.

Kevver tugged on my sleeve and pointed behind us.

I turned around and found myself nose to navel with a guy who had to be at least seven feet tall.

I looked up and swallowed. He looked down and smiled. He had green skin. Two large bolts stuck out of his neck. His face looked as if it had been stitched together by a drunken tailor.

He reached toward me with the biggest hand I had ever seen.

Chapter Ten

Igor and Sigmund Fred

My brain felt as if it had blown a fuse. My muscles refused to move. I could only stare at that huge hand, waiting for it to close around my neck.

Suddenly Igor pushed through the door and was standing next to me. His head barely reached my shoulder.

"For heaven's sake, don't be rude!" he hissed. "Shake hands with him, or there's no telling what might happen."

I swallowed hard and held out my hand. It was trembling like Jell-O in an earthquake. The tall, green man started to smile again. He took my hand, which disappeared inside his huge fist. "Good morning," he said.

His voice reminded me of last night's thunderstorm.

"Good morning," I managed to squeak.

"Michael," said my mother, "what is going on here?"

I blinked. How should I know what was going on? All I knew was that life was getting weirder by the minute. I swallowed and said, "This is Igor—you saw him last night—and his friend."

If Igor's "friend" had walked up behind me on a dark night, I would have screamed and run for my life. But the fact that we were in our kitchen, and that it was a bright, sunny morning helped to keep me in place.

Besides—it was all just an act.

Right?

My mother rose to the occasion. "So pleased to meet you," she said graciously. "Won't you both join us for breakfast?"

The thing standing behind Igor rumbled, which I took to mean yes. Igor rubbed his hands and clumped forward.

We made room for them at the table. The chair creaked under the creature's weight, but didn't break.

I wasn't sure what to call the tall green man. He sure looked like Frankenstein's monster. But I didn't want to call him "Frank." As a monster lover, I knew "Frankenstein" wasn't the name of the monster. It was the name of the scientist who made him. The correct title for the creature itself is "Frankenstein's Monster."

But that's not really a name. I mean, you wouldn't say, "Pass the butter, please, Frankenstein's monster." At least, I wouldn't—not under those circumstances.

Finally I got up my courage and said, "Aren't you going to introduce us to your friend, Igor?"

Igor looked at me as if I was out of my mind. "You mean you don't know who this is?" he asked.

"I know!" I said. "I just wasn't sure what I should call him."

Igor sighed. "That's a delicate subject," he said, slathering cream cheese on a bagel.

We all waited. Igor put down the bagel. "It's like this," he said. "The man who made my friend named him Sigmund. But he used a brain that had once belonged to a man named Fred. So sometimes we call him Sigmund. And sometimes we call him Fred. And sometimes we call him Sigmund Fred."

Kevver snorted. "That's what you get when you let some psycho analyze things."

I knew there was a joke in there somewhere, but I didn't have time to figure it out. The monster was starting to growl.

Igor looked a little nervous. "So usually I don't

call him anything," he continued quickly, "since it just upsets him."

"Just make sure you call me for dinner," rumbled the monster.

And then he smiled. The sight made me nervous. I was afraid he was going to rip out some of his stitches.

My mother laughed her business laugh—the one she uses when she doesn't want to offend a client who's just told a joke she doesn't think is very funny.

"You two are quite delightful," she said. "Now, why don't you tell us what this is all about."

Igor raised one bushy black eyebrow. "I beg your pardon?"

"Who are you working for?" she asked. "I can't believe you went to all this trouble just for the fun of it. Those costumes are terrific. Come on— you can tell us. It's not against the rules or anything. Who put you up to this?"

Igor's nostrils flared, and he raised his other eyebrow to the level of the first. "Madame," he said, in dignified tones, "We have come to enter the Monster of the Year Contest. We have come in good faith. I do not like to have our sincerity questioned."

"Well, where do you live?" asked Jeff. I had the impression he was trying to humor Igor.

"We have a cozy little castle in Transylvania."

It was my mother's turn to raise an eyebrow. "Transylvania?" she asked slyly. "I thought that was where the Count lived."

"That arrogant booby!" cried Igor. "I, too, was born and raised in Transylvania. But I had dreams, ambitions. So I moved on. After much wandering, I met—the doctor." He placed his hand over his heart. "The doctor. Ah, now there was a man."

Sigmund Fred put out one huge hand and tipped it back and forth. It was clear he didn't think as much of "the doctor" as Igor did.

"With the doctor, I scaled the heights of success. When we retired, I took Sigmund Fred back to Transylvania with me, where I bought the very castle my parents had worked in when I was a child."

My mother rolled her eyes. She thought Igor was full of baloney, and she was getting tired of it. Fortunately, the conversation was interrupted by the doorbell.

It was Skip and Lulu. When Skip saw the tall, green man sitting at our breakfast table sipping tea, the ends of his moustache began to twitch.

"See, Daddy," said Lulu. "I told you they were interesting."

"How do you do," said Skip, when we introduced our visitors. He looked so nervous when he shook hands with Fred that I almost laughed. Then I realized that I must have looked about the same way myself a few minutes back.

"Coffee?" asked my mother.

"I'd love some!" said Skip.

When Mom went to get the coffee, Skip turned to Igor and Sigmund Fred. "How would you two like to be on my show tomorrow?" he asked.

"Can we talk about the rude way we were treated at the hotel last night?" asked Igor.

"Sounds good to me," said Skip.

Mom set a cup of coffee next to him. He smiled at her and took a sip. I realized it must have been a relief to him to get a cup of coffee and be sure that Lulu hadn't had a crack at it. Unfortunately he was so interested in our visitors that he failed to keep an eye on his daughter.

"How long does it take you to do your makeup?" he asked Sigmund Fred.

"Why do we need makeup for radio?" asked Igor.

"Well, you don't," said Skip. "But I want to have a photographer there. I'd like to get you just the way you are now. You look great."

"But we are not wearing makeup," said Igor angrily.

Skip smiled and took a sip of his coffee. "Phh-auugh!" he cried, spitting it back into the cup.

Lulu covered her face with her hands and made loud, piggy laughing noises.

Igor and the monster looked confused.

"Come on, Lulu, we're going home," said Skip angrily.

I expected Lulu to complain. But I guess she figured she had had her fun for the morning, so she didn't care what happened next.

"Skip and those two were made for each other," said my mother after the Toomaloos had left.

I didn't think she meant it in a nice way. She went in the kitchen and started dragging out her cookbooks. Jeff went out to help her. Even so, I knew she was going to be in a bad mood for the rest of the day. She hates cooking—especially on Sundays. But as long as we had company, she felt she had to.

Kevver and I stayed in the living room with Igor and Sigmund Fred.

"So what did happen at the hotel last night?" I asked.

Igor frowned. "They would not accept my money," he said.

"Why not?"

He pulled a bag out of his coat. "They say it is not good," he said, emptying the bag on to the coffee table.

67

I could feel my eyes getting rounder. The bag was filled with gold coins.

"Are these real?" I asked.

"Of course they are real!" said Igor. "Genuine Transylvanian gold coins. But that fool clerk said he had never seen any such thing, and he couldn't accept them. So I took my credit card. But they didn't accept Transylvanian Express either."

Igor talked all about that on Skip's show the next morning. Later Skip helped him organize a press conference, and he repeated the story for the local papers. They loved it—especially since he had Fred with him. The seven-foot-tall green monster made a great "photo op." (That's newspaper talk for photo opportunity—the chance to get a good picture.)

I wasn't surprised when the local newspapers carried the story. They had been having a lot of fun with the Monster of the Year Contest. What I didn't expect was that the national news would pick it up. But they did, and the next day Igor and Fred were featured in newspapers, coast to coast.

That night we got a second telegram from the person who called himself the Count. He claimed to be outraged at "Fred" for traveling to America to try to pick up the Monster of the Year Award.

"Tell Igor this means war" were the last words of the telegram.

Jeff was still convinced that this was all some big publicity stunt. I wasn't so sure now. But when I woke up that night and found the biggest bat I'd ever seen in my life hovering at the foot of my bed, I made up my mind.

This was for real.

Chapter Eleven

Life Gets Weirder

I had never been so scared in my life. I lay beneath the sheets, staring out at that big bat and thinking: *This is it; I'm about to become one of the living dead.*

I also thought: *Why is it you never have a chunk of garlic when you need it?*

Suddenly the bat fluttered its wings extra fast. Everything went kind of hazy. I felt dizzy. I don't know what happened next exactly. I only remember that I heard a sound like a cork popping out of a champagne bottle.

When I could focus again, a tall, pale man was standing beside my bed. A thin mist swirled around his feet. A long black cape hung from his shoulders, and his jet black hair was slicked back from his pale face. "Good evening," he said, raising one elegant black eyebrow. "You are Michael McGraw, are you not?"

I nodded, wondering when he was going to bite my neck.

"Don't vorry—I am not going to bite your neck," he said as if he had read my mind. He had a deep voice and a funny accent that put the stress on the wrong syllable half the time. "I am here to enter your contest—and to teach those upstarts Igor and Sigmund Fred a lesson in manners. I assume you have a place for me to stay?"

"I don't know," I said. "I'll have to check with my mother."

All right: so I was too cowardly to tell him no on my own. At least I didn't tell *him* to go ask my mother.

"I assume it vill be settled quickly," he said. "I read in the news that you have offered Igor and Sigmund Fred your hospitality. If this is so, it vould not be good to refuse me. It vould make the contest appear—unfair! Especially as I contacted you *before* they did."

"You did?"

He looked at me scornfully. "You did receive my telegram, did you not?"

I remembered the telegram that arrived the day WERD had told Mom they wanted to sponsor the contest—the one signed, the Count. I swallowed. "We got it. But we didn't think it was for real."

My visitor looked offended. "Not real?" he asked in a low, dangerous voice.

"Well, no," I said. "We thought it was a joke. After all, how could you have known about the contest so early?"

"I have my sources," he said. Then I remembered the bats we had seen circling the billboard. I swallowed nervously. "What do you want me to do?" I asked.

"Tell your mother the Count has arrived," he said. "I vill avait her response."

Then he swirled his cape in front of his face. I heard the champagne cork noise again. A sudden puff of smoke hid him from view. When the air had cleared, the Count was gone and the bat was back. It fluttered into the corner, and hung upside down from the edge of my bookcase.

Keeping one eye on the bat, I slipped out of bed. I grabbed my robe, headed for the door, and ran down the hall to my parents' room.

"Mom!" I yelled. "Jeff! We've got company!"

Jeff came to the door, tying on his robe and looking groggy.

"Michael, what in heavens' name is going on?" he growled.

I swallowed. How was I going to explain this one? Finally I just said, "The Count is here."

Jeff sighed. "This is too much," he said. "I don't mind these people—whoever they are—taking advantage of your contest for a little self-promotion, but what makes them think they can disturb us in the middle of the night? This is too weird."

"Jeff, this may be weirder than you think."

"What do you mean?"

I swallowed, then said cautiously, "I think this guy is for real."

Jeff put his hands over his face. That's the gesture he makes when he's trying to figure out an important plot point. It means he's thinking really hard.

"All right," he said at last. "Let's head for the kitchen."

"Jeff, I don't think you understand. There's a vampire in my bedroom!"

"That's why we're going to the kitchen. I want to get some garlic."

"You mean you believe me?" I said in surprise.

"Let's just say that I'm keeping an open mind," he replied. "Obviously, if I was in my right mind, I would say that you were out of yours. But since I make my living by trying to believe six impossi-

73

ble things before breakfast, I can't just brush you off. So let's get some garlic. Then we'll see what's up."

To my surprise, we had a whole string of fresh garlic. "Lucky thing Mom went shopping this week," I said.

"Luck had nothing to do with it," said Jeff. "I bought that garlic myself."

I looked at him. He shrugged. "I told you, I make my living by taking the impossible seriously." He cut the rope of garlic in the middle and handed me half of it. "I also believe in being prepared. Now—tell me a little more about what happened."

I think the look on Jeff's face was even more frightening than the arrival of the Count. He didn't act as if he thought I had had a bad dream. He was taking me seriously, and he looked pretty nervous.

I don't like it when adults get scared. It makes the world seem out of control.

"Did he seem friendly?" asked Jeff when I had finished my story.

"Well, he didn't seem mean," I said. "But that doesn't necessarily tell you anything."

He nodded. We both knew plenty of people who acted nice but were really mean—and vice versa.

"He did say I didn't have to worry," I continued.

"The government says something like that every year when they send out the tax forms," replied Jeff. "Better hold on to your garlic."

And with that we started back up the stairs.

The Count had changed back into his human form. "Greetings," he said when I introduced him to Jeff. "I am so pleased to meet you." He glanced at the garlic. "I see you are feeling cautious," he added.

Jeff smiled. "It never hurts to be careful," he said.

"I disagree," replied the Count. "Sometimes diving right in is the only vay to avoid real pain. But that is neither here nor there. I vas inquiring about a place for me to stay."

Jeff scratched his head. "Don't you have a—well, a coffin, or something?" he said.

The Count nodded. "But of course. It should be delivered any moment now. I vould appreciate a room below ground, if you do not mind. The sunlight—hurts my eyes."

The doorbell rang. "Ah," said the Count. "That vill be my coffin."

Jeff looked at his watch. "A vampire I can almost believe. But deliverymen who come at three in the morning? That's the strangest thing I've heard yet."

As we followed the Count down the stairs I got the feeling that his feet were not actually touching the steps. But his cape was in the way, so I couldn't tell for certain.

We opened the door.

"Ah," said the Count, rubbing his hands together. "My home away from home."

Resting on the sidewalk was a polished wooden box, the deliverymen nowhere to be seen.

"Give me a hand, will you?" said the Count.

The coffin was lighter than it looked. I realized that was because it was empty. Working together, the three of us carried it into the cellar.

The Count was delighted when he found that the cellar had been divided into sections. "Do you have guests down here often?" he asked.

"Not really," said Jeff.

The Count poked his head into the cubicles until he found one that he liked. "Vell, it's not the Plaza," he said. "But I guess it vill do for now." He glanced around. "Vould you mind terribly finding something to cover those windows?"

Jeff found some burlap sacks and we tacked them up over the windows.

"Thank you kindly," said the Count. He lifted the lid of his coffin. "Such a cozy spot," he said, looking into it. "If you vill forgive me, I am exhausted from my journey. I vill visit vith you more tomorrow."

"But not before sunset, eh?" asked Jeff.

The count lifted one long eyebrow. "Vhat do you think?" he asked with a smile.

The curve of his lip revealed a pair of gleaming fangs.

Chapter Twelve

And Weirder!

"Well, what *do* you think?" I asked Jeff when we were back upstairs.

"I think life is weirder than anyone can imagine."

"Come on, Jeff. You know what I mean. Is he for real?"

Jeff laughed. "You're the one who saw him turn into a bat," he said.

That was true. But I was beginning to wonder if it had been some kind of trick. I was pretty groggy when he first woke me up. Maybe he had hypnotized me, or something. It didn't seem likely. But then, how likely was it that we just helped a vampire drag his coffin into our cellar?

I didn't sleep very well that night. It was a big relief when morning came.

The relief didn't last long. As I came down to breakfast I heard an angry voice in the kitchen.

"Here?" cried Igor in astonishment. "You let him come here?"

I came through the door in time to see my mother smack a large spoon against the table. The noise made Sigmund Fred flinch.

"Now you listen here, Mr. Igor," said Mom. "This is *our* house, and it is *our* business who we let stay here."

"But we are enemies," said Igor. "We are having a feud."

"Well, have your feud somewhere else," said Mom.

Good old Mom. She wasn't taking any nonsense from these monsters. Sometimes it pays to have a hard-nosed advertising executive around the house.

I slipped into a chair beside Sigmund Fred. "Have some cereal," he rumbled, passing me a box of flakes. The box looked tiny inside his giant green hand. It was almost empty. That was because the monster had already taken most of it. He was eating out of a mixing bowl, and using one of Mom's big cooking spoons to shovel the cereal into his mouth. I noticed the bolts at the side of his head moving up and down as he chewed. I hoped one of them would fall off. At least that would prove he was a fake.

But they stayed right in place.

It was a relief when two guys from the radio station arrived to pick up Igor and Sigmund Fred. Since we could count on the Count to sleep until sunset—or at least, to pretend to do so—we could stop worrying about the monsters until after supper.

The Count appeared about five minutes after sunset, looking for V-8 juice.

I found a can at the back of the pantry.

"Sorry it's not cold," I said.

The Count shivered. "That vould be terrible," he replied. "I much prefer it varm."

He watched as I rummaged in the drawer for a can opener. "That tool is much like a big fang, isn't it?" he said as I poked a hole in the top of the can.

"I hadn't noticed that until you mentioned it," I said. I poured some of the thick, red juice into a glass and passed it to him.

He licked his lips. "Vould you happen to have a straw?" he asked. "It seems more natural if I can —suck it."

I found a straw, and the Count went into the living room. Unfortunately, the guys from WERD chose that moment to bring Igor and Sigmund Fred back to the house.

"Ah, I see the peasants have returned," said the

Count, who was leaning against the fireplace, sucking on his V-8 juice. "How charming."

"This is America," snapped Igor. "Everyone is a peasant here. So being a Count doesn't count for a thing."

"So clever!" purred the Count. "And so short!"

Fred started to rumble about then. The noise started somewhere deep inside him. It began to get louder and louder, like an approaching jet airplane.

"Why doesn't everyone come to dinner!" said my mother, desperately trying to sound cheerful.

Igor and the Count managed to avoid an actual fight during the meal. Mostly they just sneered at each other.

"Look," said my mother. "Are we being filmed or something? Is this like some big joke?"

Igor, Fred, and the Count looked offended. But before anyone could answer, the doorbell rang.

By this time that was getting to be pretty frightening in and of itself.

For a minute no one said a thing.

The bell rang again.

"Oh, go answer it," said my mother. But she didn't sound happy.

When I opened the door, I knew her mood was only going to get worse.

Standing on the front step was a tall creature

H. Kurtz

covered with green scales. He had webbed hands, and gills at the side of his head. A puddle of water had collected around his big, flat feet.

"Hi," he said with a nervous smile. "I'm the Creature from the Yuccky Lagoon. Have I come to the right place?"

I hesitated for a moment, then invited the creature in. By this point, I thought, what difference did it make?

The creature spotted the aquarium on the other side of the room and said, "Oh, do you raise your own food?"

"Actually, those are just to look at," I said.

The creature glanced at me like I was out of my mind. But he shrugged and said, "I'm so excited about your contest. I think it may be just the break I need to get back into the business."

"You'll never get back into the business," said a voice behind me. "You've got no talent."

It was Igor. He was crouched in the doorway leading to the kitchen. Fred and the Count loomed large behind him.

"That's not true!" cried the scaly creature. He sounded hurt. "I had lousy scripts. I had bad directors and low budgets. But that doesn't mean I got no talent. All I needed was a good agent."

At the mention of the word *agent* the other three made a series of gestures with their hands, crossing them in front of their faces a couple of times, then spitting between their fingers.

"What was that all about?" I asked.

"It's a protective ritual," said Igor.

Before I could figure out what he was talking about, someone knocked on the door.

I hesitated. Did I really want to answer it?

"Oh, go ahead," said Jeff, who had elbowed his way through the monsters. "We might as well see what happens next."

That's one of the neat things about having a science-fiction writer for a father; he tends to look at life as a kind of story.

I was almost disappointed when the person who knocked on the door seemed so normal. He was a bit taller than average, with sandy brown hair. The only thing that looked a little odd were his eyebrows, which were so thick and bushy that they merged into a single long brow stretching right across his forhead.

"Is this the place to come for the monster contest?" he asked. He sounded kind of nervous.

"It seems to be be," I said. "Come on in."

He stepped into the living room.

"Vell, I suppose it vas about time for one of his kind to show up," said the Count.

"I don't understand," I said. "What are you doing here? You don't look like a monster."

"Just wait," grumbled Igor. "We've got a few more nights until the moon is full.

Suddenly everything clicked. I remembered what I had read about people who had the kind of long, thick eyebrow this guy had.

"You!" I cried. "You're a werewolf!"

Chapter Thirteen

Judge Not, Lest Ye Be Clobbered!

The man nodded and bobbed his head. "That's all right, isn't it? I mean, werewolves do get to enter your contest, don't they?"

"I suppose it depends on whether or not the moon is full the night of the contest," I said. He was so gentle and—well, nervous, I guess—that it was hard to imagine him in a monster contest. But then, who knew what he would be like once the moon was full?

"Now look, fellows," said my mother, who had followed Jeff into the living room. "I want to know why you've all come here. I'm not preju- diced or anything. But I really don't want my house full of monsters. Surely with the careers you've had, you have enough money to go to a hotel or something."

"They don't want us," said the Frankenstein monster sadly.

"That's right," said Igor. "They do not . . ."

Suddenly he seemed to sag. "Oh, let's be honest," he said. "Most of us aren't very well off these days. The business has changed. Fifty years ago we were the kings. The greatest ever. We had heart. People loved us even when they were afraid of us. But it's not that way anymore. The new guys are different. Guys like Jason and Freddy Krueger have taken over the business. Siggie and I were hoping this contest might change things a little. I guess the others all had the same idea."

It made me sad to hear him talk like that. I mean, I loved these guys. I thought they were they greatest.

"Ve have been tossed into the trashbin of pop culture," said the Count gloomily.

"It's not true," I cried. "Lots of people still love you!"

The Count's lower lip started to tremble. For a second, I thought he was going to cry. I hoped he wouldn't; then I wondered if he could. It seemed like one of those things that vampires couldn't do—like casting a reflection in a mirror.

The mirror! I glanced at the one which hung in the hall. Sigmund Fred and Igor were standing right beside it, their reflections clear in the slightly dusty glass. But the Count had positioned himself so that he was nowhere near it.

Had he done that on purpose? I still couldn't tell if these guys were for real or not.

"I suppose we can put you all up for the time being," said Jeff. He sounded a little nervous. I wondered if he was worried about sleeping in a house with all these monsters—or about what my mother was going to say when she got him alone.

She didn't wait to get him alone. "Now just hold on," she said. "Before we invite them to stay here, I want to know who these people really are."

Igor drew himself up to his full four and a half feet. "Madam, we are just what we say we are: monsters—or in my case, a friend of a monster —who happen to be down on our luck."

"No, I mean who are you *really*," persisted my mother. She turned to the Creature from the Yuccky Lagoon. "You, take off your mask so I can see what's underneath."

The creature looked worried. "I'm not wearing a mask," he said.

My mother put on her no-nonsense face and went over to examine him. "There must be a zipper here someplace," she said. "I've seen those movies. You can always see the zipper in one of these costumes."

"They used to put on a fake zipper, so people

would think I wasn't real," said the creature. "The director thought it was more believable that way."

"Directors!" cried the others in disgust. They made that series of hand gestures again, ending with a "P-tooie" between their fingers. It was a good thing they were doing a dry-spit. Otherwise Mom would have been very angry.

"Jeff," said my mother nervously, "you're the specialist in weirdness. You handle this."

"All right. Look, guys," said Jeff. "All I want is a promise that we'll be safe with you around."

"I never bite my hosts!" cried the Count, sounding terribly offended.

"Well, we don't want you biting anyone else in the area, either," I said.

The Count nodded. "Medical science has made great strides regarding my—condition. If you will simply provide me with plenty of the elixir of life, I can guarantee my behavior."

"The elixir of life?" said my mother nervously. "You mean you want us to get you *blood*?"

"No," said The Count. "V-8 juice. I need lots of V-8 juice."

Now, I ask you—what do you do with a vampire like that?

My mother had much the same question, which

is why she hauled us to the radio station the next morning.

When we got there, Skip was skipping. I mean it. He was holding the morning paper, which had another front page article about the contest, and he was hopping around outside the sound booth singing, "This is great. This is incredible. This is wo-o-o-o-nderful."

"This is annoying," said my mother. "Look, Skip, I have a demented dwarf and his seven-foot friend sleeping in my spare bedroom, a gill man soaking in my bathtub, a vampire in the cellar, and a werewolf in my attic. At least, that was the total when we left his morning. Who knows how many there may be when we get back?"

Kevver started to speak up. I nudged him into silence. This was *not* the time to mention the Mummy that had showed up at midnight, asking for a place to "rest his weary bones."

Skip stopped and looked at my mother. "Aren't you having fun?" he asked.

"Fun?" my mother exploded. "Fun! Skip, I have a business to run. I have a child to raise. I can't cope with any more monsters."

"You should try raising Lulu," said Skip ruefully.

"Lulu is your problem!" cried my mother. She grabbed the front of Skip's jacket and pulled him forward until their noses were almost touching.

"Listen, Toomaloo: I can't spend all my time feeding monsters."

The tips of Skip's moustache started to twitch. "I'll see if I can get the station to help out," he said.

Which was the beginning of the night I still think of as The Great Restaurant Disaster.

It started out well enough. At Skip's urging, Station WERD decided to treat the monsters to dinner at a fancy French restaurant called Chez Stadium. The management was a little hazy about exactly who they were, but as long as they were getting good publicity out of it, they didn't mind.

My mother was jealous. Chez Stadium was one of her favorite restaurants. She was also a little nervous, since she sometimes took her clients there.

"Please don't embarrass me, boys," she said as we were getting ready to leave. "This is a very high-tone establishment." She straightened my tie, which I had been told I MUST wear, and used a little spit to slick down my hair.

"Oh, calm down," said Jeff. "It'll do those stiffs good to have someone a little different come to dinner."

I looked around at our crew. Different was hardly the word. At seven-thirty a stretch limousine pulled up outside the house. Nine of us climbed into the car: me, Kevver, the six monsters who had already been there, plus a hunchback named Quasimodo. "Quaz," as he suggested we call him, had arrived just after sunset. At first he and Igor had stared at each other suspiciously. But when Quaz found out that Igor was not going to be a contestant, he seemed to relax.

Mom and Jeff stood on the porch and waved as we drove off. They were holding hands. I think they were looking forward to an evening alone.

Skip and Lulu met us at the restaurant. It was a good thing Skip had warned the management ahead of time. Otherwise I don't think we would have gotten in.

The restaurant wasn't the only place Skip had warned. Several of the local TV stations had sent camera crews.

"How do you think I got them to let us come?" whispered Skip when I asked about it. "Chez Stadium was *not* interested in having a group of monsters come to dinner. But when I explained the publicity angle, they changed their minds."

Publicity again. Everyone wanted publicity.

The TV crews had attracted a crowd. Everybody was waving and cheering as we made our way into the restaurant. A tall man in a tuxedo greeted us at the door.

"Walk this way," he said and sniffed.

As we followed him into the dining room I noticed that Kevver was holding his shoulders very straight. He had his nose in the air.

"What are you doing?" I asked.

"The waiter said, 'Walk this way,' " said Kevver.

I poked him in the ribs and reminded him that my mother wanted us to behave.

As it turned out, it wasn't Kevver I needed to worry about.

The maître d' (that's what they called the guy in the tux who took us to our seats) showed us to a large round table under a huge chandelier. A starched white cloth covered the table.

When I sat down and looked at my plate I got nervous. It was surrounded by more silverware than I usually use in a day. I remembered the rule my mother gave me: Start at the outside, and work your way in. That was good as far as it went. But what was I supposed to do with the fork at the top of my plate?

"Get a load of that," said Kevver, pointing behind us with his thumb.

I glanced over my shoulder. In the center of the room was a two-level table. It was loaded with more fancy desserts that I had ever seen in my life—thick pies, cream puffs, cakes with so many layers I couldn't even count them. I would have been glad to skip supper and just have dessert.

Dinner started with appetizers. The Count ordered V-8 juice. The lagoon man asked for raw clams. The Mummy wanted some dry toast. Quasimodo did what I really wanted to do, and asked for a French pastry.

As for Lulu, she ordered some of everything.

When everyone had settled in, Skip raised his water glass. "I'd like to propose a toast," he said. "Here's to the judges of the first Monster of the Year Contest: Kevver Smith and Michael McGraw."

A deathly silence fell over the table. Every one of those monsters turned toward me and Kevver. Suddenly I realized just what we'd gotten ourselves into. We were going to have to pick one of them to win the contest.

That meant we were going to make one monster very happy.

It also meant we were going to make the rest of them very, very angry.

Chapter Fourteen

Disaster at Dinner

It was Lulu who broke the awful silence. "I'm sure glad I'm not you guys," she said.

She sounded really happy.

I decided silence would have been better.

Suddenly I noticed that the lagoon creature was weeping. His tears were green, as if they had algae in them. They rolled down his scaly cheeks and fell into his raw clams.

"What's wrong?" I asked, putting a hand on his arm. I could feel the muscles move and shift under his leathery green skin. It was kind of frightening. But it was hard to be too frightened of someone who was so unhappy.

"I don't have a chance," he cried. "I shouldn't even be here. The others don't like me. They never have. They say I'm just an upstart, not a classic like them."

It was meant to be a quiet conversation between the two of us. But Lulu had ears that the government should study for use in spy planes. When she heard what the creature said, she decided to help, in her own revolting way.

"Is that true?" she demanded. "Have you guys been picking on Swamp Lips here?"

The other monsters looked embarrassed. They stared at their plates and poked their food around.

"It's not really him," said the Count at last. "It's just that he made so many lousy movies he started giving monsters a bad name."

"It wasn't my fault," blubbered the creature. "It was the scripts. I had lousy writers."

"Writers!" cried the others in disgust. They made that complicated gesture, and spit through their fingers again. I was glad Jeff wasn't here to see *that*.

A passing waiter did happen to notice. I thought for a minute he was going to throw us out of the restaurant. But we were a pretty big group, and I guess he decided he didn't want to lose the tip. Or maybe it was the thought of what might happen to someone who tried to throw us out. The idea would have made me think twice!

The lagoon creature's bad feelings seemed to loosen something up in the other monsters. They all started to talk about the past.

"We've each had our share of hard times," said

Quaz, in his gravelly voice. "Remember when the Mummy and I had that fight over a girl we were both in love with?"

"I remember!" roared Fred. "You grabbed his bandages and started to run. It's a good thing you can't run very fast, or there would have been nothing left of him." He started to laugh, which made the whole table shake.

"I didn't think it was funny," said the Mummy dryly. "I was dizzy for a month."

The Count started to chuckle. "How about the time Igor put the starch in your hairspray, Volfie? I haven't laughed that hard in years."

"That wasn't funny either," replied the Wolfman stiffly. "In fact, I thought it was quite disrespectful."

"Ooo," said the Count, shaking his fingers daintily "Aren't ve la-di-da all of a sudden?"

"Well, what makes you think you're so great?" Lulu asked the Count. "I've seen your old movies. I think you should have gone to acting school."

Sigmund Fred start to snort and pound the table. "She got you, Count," he wheezed happily. The rest of us snatched our glasses, which were wildly bouncing around from the whacking he was giving the table.

"And I suppose you call vhat you did acting, Siggie?" replied the Count. "All that grunting and groaning! You sounded like you vere doing barnyard imitations."

"Now, boys," said Skip.

The monsters ignored him.

Lulu ignored him, too, which was unfortunate, since she was the one who got things stirred up. "I always liked the Mummy best, anyway," she said. I doubt she had even seen a film with the Mummy. She just wanted to annoy the others.

The Mummy smiled gratefully.

"That stuffed shirt!" cried Igor. "He couldn't scare up ten cents to make a phone call."

"Hey!" cried the Mummy.

"Being scary isn't the only thing in life," interrupted Quasimodo. "I touched people's hearts."

"Yeah, and I've got a hunch that's why you only got one story," said Igor. "They couldn't figure out what to do with you so they kept making the same film over and over. *Ding dong, ding dong!* All those bells in that old church. If you had been versatile, like me, you might have been in lots of films."

"Lots of *cheap* films," said Quasimodo. "Rip-offs of rip-offs. You aren't a character. You're a cliche!"

"Now, boys," said Skip again. Everyone ignored him. So he took a sip of coffee. Then he spit it back in his cup and glared at Lulu, who was trying to look innocent.

"A cliche?" cried Igor. "Look, Buster, there's room for only one hunchback in this monster business, and I'm it."

And then he hit him with his spoon.

At that point I expected Quasimodo to pick Igor up and throw him across the room. Instead he started to cry, which made two of them, since the Creature from the Yucky Lagoon was still leaking tears, too.

The lagoon creature was sympathetic to Quasimodo. I think it had something to do with them both feeling like second class monsters. Anyway, while Quaz didn't respond, Goony did. He stood up and flicked Igor on the ear. "You leave him alone!" he said sternly.

"Did you see that?" cried Igor. "Did you see what he did?"

"No, I missed it," said Lulu, an evil twinkle in her eyes. "What did he do?"

"Are you out of your mind?" I hissed at her. "What are you trying to do, cause a riot?"

"It is one of my life's goals," she said. Her voice was so sincere I couldn't help but believe her. I didn't know what to say. It didn't matter, because about that time war broke out.

"Don't you touch my friend!" roared the Franken-

stein monster. He grabbed a ketchup bottle and shook it at Quasimodo.

Now you know as well as I do that shaking a ketchup bottle is usually about as effective as kicking a rock. But you have to remember who was shaking it. With a loud *kuh-loop* a huge glob of ketchup went flying across the table. It splattered across Quasimodo's tunic.

"Yum!" cried the Count when he saw the red smear. Leaping to his feet, he dived for the Quaz. Then he caught himself. "Excuse me," he said, looking truly embarrassed. "I got carried away."

Quasimodo had also gotten carried away, because he picked up his French pastry, pointed it at Fred, and squashed it between his hands. This caused a great chunk of white cream to go flying across the table. However it missed Fred completely. In fact, it missed everyone at our table. Instead it landed on the throat of an elegant lady sitting a table away and began dripping down the front of her dress.

"Oh!" she shrieked. "Oh, oh, oh!"

Lulu was laughing so hard she nearly fell off her chair.

The woman's husband (or her boyfriend, or whatever) glared at us. Then he picked up his soupbowl. Carrying it over to our table, he poured it into Quasimodo's lap.

"You can't do that!" shouted the lagoon creature. "He's my friend." He grabbed his raw clams
and started stuffing them down the man's neck.

"Go, Goony!" cried Lulu. By this time she was
laughing so hard she couldn't control herself. I
watched in astonishment as she really did fall off
her chair.

The excitement was too much for the Wolfman.
Even though he was still in human form, he
climbed on his chair and started to howl. The
woman sitting behind him began to scream. He
turned toward her and began clacking his teeth
together.

"Now, boys!" said Skip. "I think you'd better—"

But before he could tell us what he thought, a
flying chicken breast hit him in the face. *Sploop!*
The meat fell to the floor, leaving Skip with gooey
sauce dripping from this moustache. "Stop it!" he
ordered, wiping away the sauce. "Stop it right
now!"

It was about then that someone discovered the
dessert cart. When the first lemon meringue pie
took flight, I knew we were in for a rough time. It
sailed across the room and hit the snooty maître
d' in the face.

"*Sacre bleu!*" he cried. But his fake French accent disappeared as he ran for the fire extinguisher.

"You want foam!" he shrieked. "I'll give you foam!"

He turned the canister upside down and shook it. A stream of white foam flooded the floor. People were slipping and sliding all over the place. Next to me a beautiful lady in a red strapless gown fell face-down into her onion soup.

"Stop this!" cried the Frankenstein monster. He stood up—a seven-foot tower of green muscle— and smashed his hand into the table for silence.

The main effect of this action was to smash the table into the floor.

By now the air was thick with pies. Suddenly a cream puff went sailing past my ear. I looked up and saw Igor swinging from the crystal chandelier. He had an armful of cream puffs, and he was lobbing them across the room like hand grenades: *Splat! Splat! Splat!* Gobs of cream were erupting all around us.

As the chandelier hit the peak of its swing a well-dressed lady with raspberries in her hair went screaming past the table. That was more than the Wolfman could stand. He went bounding after her, snapping at her heels—which looked pretty strange, since he was still completely human.

"This is the best night of my life!" cried Lulu. She was rolling around on the floor, holding her sides and shrieking with laughter.

Suddenly I heard a noise like the pop of a champagne cork. The Count had disappeared.

"Oh, my God!" cried a lady on the other side of the room. "There's a bat in here! A bat! A bat!"

People started screaming. Women in fancy dresses covered their heads and ran for the door. Unfortunately the police arrived before any of them could get out. The screaming got louder. Kevver and I crawled under a table to watch what happened next.

We might have escaped the police roundup if Sigmund Fred hadn't decided to join us.

With the table floating two feet in the air, it was easy for the cops to find us.

Chapter Fifteen

Gadzinga!

My mother had to come down to the police station to get us out. She was not amused. She was even less happy when she saw the morning paper. Actually, *disgusted* was the word she used—as in, "I'm disgusted with all of you."

This was her first statement at breakfast the next morning. Her second was: "I can't believe you acted so childishly."

Mothers must have some secret power to instill guilt. Only two sentences, and she had those monsters hanging their heads in shame. I was feeling guilty, and I hadn't even done anything.

"We're sorry, Ms. Adams," everyone muttered. Well, everyone except the lagoon creature. He had taken to calling my mother "Mom." He looked up at her and said, "It won't happen again, Mom." He sounded miserable.

My mother looked uncomfortable. She was still

trying to figure out how to deal with Goony. "Well, I should hope not," she said at last. "You may be even sorrier when you see the effect of your actions. Listen to *this* headline: 'Smud Renames BAM! Vows All Out War on Monsters.'"

It turned out that Myrna Smud had been having dinner at Chez Stadium when the pie fight broke out. My theory is she only showed up to keep an eye on us. Well, she got an eyeful all right—an eyeful of lemon meringue pie. She had been so offended by the whole thing that she called the newspapers to announce BAM! had been changed from "Billboards Are Monstrous!" to "Ban All Monsters!" She was starting a petition to have the city council outlaw monsters in Syracuse.

"She can't do that!" cried Igor. "It's discrimination!"

"Never underestimate the power of a small mind," said Jeff sadly.

"What are we going to do?" moaned the wolfman. He was holding an ice pack against a large lump on his head, which he had gotten when someone bonked him during the battle in the restaurant.

"I'd suggest you start by trying to behave," said my mother. "I have a feeling things are going to get worse before they get better. Here's the third article I wanted you to hear."

And then she read a ridiculous item about rumors that a radioactive dinosaurlike creature was swimming his way up the Great Lakes, and was scheduled to arrive in town the next morning.

"Gadzinga!" cried the lagoon creature happily. "He's my hero!"

"That's absurd!" said Igor. "This isn't his kind of contest."

"That doesn't make any difference," said Mom. "When people get upset, rumors start to fly. But I would like to get my hands on the idiot who started this rumor. We've got enough troubles as it is."

A nervous look twitched across Jeff's face, and I got a pretty good idea where the rumor had come from. I figured he had been having a little fun at the newspapers' expense. But I wasn't about to blow the whistle on him. He's kept his mouth shut for my sake plenty of times in the past.

I forgot about the rumor until that evening when the doorbell rang. We all looked at one another nervously. Over the last week and a half answering the door had become a real adventure.

"I vill get it," said the Count at last.

We all crowded in behind him. I didn't know what to expect: another monster, a policeman, an angry BAMmer. It might have been anyone.

But it was just the UPS man. "Package for Michael McGraw," he said. "Signature required."

I pushed past the Count and signed my name on the deliveryman's clipboard. He handed me a cardboard box—a cube, about a foot and a half on each side.

"What is it?" cried everyone.

"I don't know," I said. "I haven't opened it yet!"

I carried the box into the kitchen and set it on the table. Jeff handed me a knife.

I was about to cut the packing tape when something began pounding on the sides of the box—from the inside.

I put down the knife.

"I'm not sure I want to open this," I said.

"Oh, please," cried Goony. "My curiosity is killing me."

I looked at my mother. She looked at Jeff. He just shrugged. "You've got plenty of friends here to protect you," he said. "Besides, maybe it's just a little bunny or something."

"The way things are going, it'll be a killer rabbit from Mars," I said.

But I cut the package open. As I was pulling back the flaps something leapt through the top of the box. It landed on the table, legs flexed, ready to jump again. I looked, blinked, and looked again.

A teeny-tiny *Tyrannosaurus rex* was stomping across our table. "Oh, dat better!" it growled in a

voice ten times too big for such a little creature. "Gadzinga didn't like dat box!"

Jeff gulped. "Gadzinga?" he said nervously. "I thought you were just a rumor."

"Do I look like a rumor, baldy?" roared the little monster.

Jeff blushed, and not because Gadzinga had called him baldy. I was sure now that he had started the rumor about Gadzinga—and gotten caught in the kind of reality game he had warned me about earlier.

"What are you doing in a box?" I asked. "I heard you were going to swim your way here."

"What are you, nuts?" cried the little monster. "That would take years."

Goony stared at the newcomer in horror. "Gadzinga?" he whispered. "That little thing is Gadzinga?"

"Yah, me Gadzinga. You got a problem with dat?"

"But you're so—so small," said Goony. He turned away, and I heard him whisper, "All my life I've looked up to Gadzinga. And now I find out he's only eighteen inches tall!" He sounded crushed.

"It's what's inside dat counts," roared Gadzinga. Stomping across the table, he opened his mouth and shot out a heat ray.

"Ouch!" cried Igor.

The Quaz patted Goony's back consolingly.

The Count was less sympathetic. "You should have known they always use miniatures in those movies," he said.

"Excuse me," said Goony. "I think I need to go upstairs and soak in the bathtub for a while." Shoulders drooping, he trudged out of the room.

"Another dream crushed by reality," said the Quaz. "The world is full of heartbreak."

"Heartbreak, schmeartbreak." said Igor. "He'll get over it. In the meantime we've got to figure out some way to get people around here on our side."

"What we need is a public relations campaign," I said. "You know about that stuff, Mom. Can't we figure out some way to get people to be glad the monsters are in town?"

My mother can't resist a professional challenge. "That's not a bad idea, Mike. If we can get people to think positively about the guys, it might take care of the whole situation."

"Maybe you could get them a Broadway show," said a tall, masked phantomlike figure who had arrived late the night before. "It worked for me."

My mother waved her hand. "That takes years," she said.

"How about endorsements?" asked Kevver. "One

of the car dealers is advertising 'monstrous savings.' Maybe the guys could do some image building that way."

"Kevver, that's brilliant!" said Mom.

"You want us to do commercials?" cried Igor. His voice sounded like he was in pain. "You want us to sell out?"

"Sell out what?" asked the Count. "A commercial couldn't be any worse than your last three movies."

"You could go the education route," said Jeff.

We all looked at him.

He shrugged and spread jam on his toast. Before he could raise it to his mouth, Gadzinga stomped over and took a bite. "Yum!" he roared. Jeff looked startled, but he kept his cool. "Look," he said, "if you really want to change the way people think, you've got to start young. So why not have the gang make guest appearances in some of the local schools?"

Chapter Sixteen

Monsters in the Classroom

My mother called the principal of the junior high where Kevver and I go, and asked if he would be interested in having the monsters visit.

"Are you kidding?" he cried. "I've got four hundred monsters in this school already. Why would I want any more?"

Fortunately, Miss Shelley, principal of our old elementary school, was more interested. So the next morning Frankenstein's monster, the Wolfman, the Creature from the Yucky Lagoon, Gadzinga, and the rest headed over to give an assembly.

The only one who didn't come was the Count; he still refused to appear before dark.

Most of the monsters were excited. Goony, however, was a nervous wreck.

"Kids make me nervous," he explained while we walked. "They're very frightening."

"Hey," I said. "*I'm* a kid!"

"But there's only one of you. Bunches of kids terrify me. Especially live ones!"

"Don't worry," said Igor. "They won't be living long once you start to talk. You'll bore them to death in the first ten minutes."

Goony turned to me. "See what I mean," he said, his lip quivering. "I don't get no respect. No never."

"Well, this is your chance to start building a new reputation," said Kevver. "If you let them in-spect you today, maybe they will re-spect you tomorrow."

The monsters groaned. Luckily, we reached the school before Kevver could make another bad joke.

"Look!" cried Goony happily. "They want us!"

He was pointing to a huge banner that hung over the front door. "Welcome to Bram Stoker Elementary," it said, in bright red letters.

Miss Shelley was waiting to greet us. "it's nice to have you back for a visit," she said to Kevver and me. "I'm very glad that you were able to bring your friends with you."

She didn't seem at all startled by the sight of the monsters. But then, as Jeff had pointed out the night before, there probably wasn't much that *could* surprise the principal of an elementary school.

"I've worked up a complete schedule for the day," said Miss Shelley, patting a stray hair back in place. "We'll start with an all-student assembly in the auditorium. I'd like each of you to talk a little bit about your career. You know, explain what you do and how you got involved in it."

The monsters looked a little uncomfortable. Miss Shelley didn't seem to notice.

"After that, we'll be sending you to individual classrooms," she continued.

Miss Shelley had everything worked out. Sigmund Fred was supposed to make a presentation on what it was like to live in a castle. The Mummy was to give a lecture an ancient history. She had assigned Goony to talk to some kids who were studying swamp life. The others were just supposed to go from class to class, doing question-and-answer sessions.

The assembly started out fairly well. Sigmund Fred titled his talk "A Patchwork Life." The Mummy told some pharaoh jokes. ("He certainly has a dry sense of humor," said Kevver.) Goony trembled and stammered, but managed to tell the story of how he was discovered by some people making a travel movie about the Yuccky Lagoon. In fact, everything went fine, until it was Gadzinga's turn. The tiny Tyrannosaurus stomped to the front of the stage, jumped onto the desk

115

next to the microphone and roared, "Me Gadzinga. Me the greatest!"

Then he offered to wrestle "any teacher in the joint."

Miss Shelley decided it was time to end the assembly. As the kids filed out, she gave each of the monsters their schedules. I should have realized that splitting them up was a mistake; it was going to make it that much harder for Kevver and I to keep things under control. When Miss Shelley told us she had invited one of the local TV stations to come in and tape part of the day for the evening news, I should have recognized that we had all the ingredients we needed for a master disaster.

Goony was still pretty nervous, so he asked me to stick with him. His speech was going pretty well when the Quaz came shuffling through the door shouting, "Trouble. Trouble in one-thirteen!"

Without waiting for Goony, I shot out of the room and raced down the hall after the Quaz. Kevver was just ahead of me. We burst into the room to find fifty third graders shouting, "I-gor! I-gor! Igor!"

Igor was standing on top of the teacher's desk, trying to fend off the kids, who were grabbing at him and holding out papers for him to autograph. He looked terrified.

"I-gor! they shouted, waving their papers at him I-gor! I-gor!"

"Get me outta here!" cried Igor when he saw me.

The kids started grabbing at him as if he were some kind of rock star. Suddenly Igor panicked. He leaped from the teacher's desk to the blackboard. Then he scrambled up the board and jumped from there to one of the support beams that ran across the ceiling.

The kids began to shout and cheer.

Grabbing the beam with his stubby hands, Igor swung his feet up, then he hung from the ceiling, quaking in terror until the teacher got the kids back in their seats.

When he climbed back down I noticed that he had left his footprint on the ceiling.

I also noticed that the newsmen had captured the whole thing on film.

Miss Shelley decided it was time for us to leave.

When the Count heard how our day had gone he laughed so hard he nearly choked on his V-8 juice. Unfortunately, Myrna Smud wasn't nearly so amused. The television cameras had captured the disaster, and they showed plenty of footage on the news that night. Naturally, they asked Myrna for her reaction.

Her response was true to form. "These terrible people are warping the minds of our young people!" she declared "They are twisting the very fabric of American society. They must be banned!"

"Vhy does that voman hate us so much?" asked the Count.

"Maybe she was scared by a monster movie when she was a little kid," said Kevver.

"I was scared by a monster movie when I was a little kid," I said. "I loved it."

My mother couldn't decide whether she was appalled or ecstatic to have her company connected to all this madness. "There's no such thing as bad publicity," she kept whispering to herself.

"Shhh!" hissed Jeff. "I want to hear what Myrna's saying."

We turned out attention back to the screen.

"I have decided that we must take vigorous action to end this menace," said Myrna. "Therefore, I am announcing that BAM! will lead an anti-monster parade past city hall tomorrow night. All concerned citizens are welcome to join us to help root this menace from our society."

"Just what is it about the monsters that bothers you so much, Mrs. Smud?" asked the interviewer.

Myrna's features puckered into her lemon-eating

look. "They overstimulate children's imaginations," she said. "This causes them to think too much, which is not healthy at a young age."

We looked at one another in astonishment. The Count rose to his feet, trembling with anger. He stood in front of the television.

"This," he said, "means var!"

Chapter Seventeen

What a Riot!

Myrna scheduled her parade for the same time as the Monster of the Year Contest. Fortunately, I didn't have time to worry about it, since both events were less than twenty-four hours away.

By six o'clock the next night it was clear that we were going to have perfect Halloween weather —cool, but not too cold; clear, with a few wispy clouds. A soft breeze was scratching the dry leaves along the sidewalks, whispering through those leaves still clinging to the trees.

We began gathering for the parade at seven-thirty. Skip had invited Jeff to lead the parade in his hearse. Kevver and I were riding in a Station WERD car close behind. It was a black convertible. The top was down, and Skip told us to sit on top of the backseat, so that we could wave to the crowds. We were real excited, until he told us Lulu was going to ride with us.

"What can I do?" said Skip apologetically. "Lulu thinks you two are wonderful." He shifted the bullhorn he was using to organize the parade from one hand to the other, then looked at it as if he might find something to say written inside its bell. "Last night she threatened to hold her breath and turn blue unless we adopted both of you. I had to call a lawyer and get him to tell her why it was impossible before she would settle down."

What could we say? I mean, how do you tell a man that his child is revolting?

Besides, he already knew.

The plan was to have the parade go south on Salina Street, turn and pass City Hall and then move on up to the War Memorial Building, where WERD was sponsoring a giant party for anyone who wanted to come. Skip had booked a pair of local bands—Squashed Spider and the Pink Punks —to play. Admission was free, but you had to pay for your own cider and doughnuts.

At the end of the night we would have the contest.

And then Kevver and I would have to make our dangerous decision. As Jeff said, the idea "was not a pretty prospect."

It wasn't just the idea of having a dozen or so monsters mad at us that bothered me. (Though that was pretty frightening.)

It was that I had gotten so fond of all of them that I couldn't stand the thought of hurting their feelings. I knew Goony would cry buckets if he lost. Quaz wouldn't cry, but his lip would tremble, and I would know that he felt terribly rejected. The Mummy would cough dryly and say, "Oh, don't mind me."

The others might hold it inside, but they would be just as upset

"What are we going to do?" I asked as we climbed into the parade car.

"I don't know," said Kevver. He looked as worried as I felt.

"I'm really scared," I said.

He nodded. "Me, too."

Then we stopped talking, because Lulu pushed in and sat between us. "Hi, guys!" she said cheerfully. "Isn't this fun? Did you bring anything to eat?"

"Sorry, Lulu," I said. "I lost my appetite two days ago."

It was the first time I ever saw sympathy in that round, red face. I guess from Lulu's point of view, losing your appetite was the worst thing that could possibly happen to you. "Oh, that's really sad," she said.

Except for Igor and Sigmund Fred, who were riding together, each monster had a convertible to himself. Several of them stopped to say hello to us as they took their places. I could tell by the look in their eyes that they were wondering if we had already made up our minds who was going to be the Monster of the Year.

If only I knew!

The parade started. The sidewalks were crammed with people, most of them in costume. It was neat seeing all those wolfmen, vampires and Frankenstein monsters when we had the real thing riding behind us.

By this time our picture had been in the paper so much that, in Syracuse at least, Kevver and I were real celebrities. Everyone cheered as we rode by.

"Wow!" I said. "They like us!"

"I'm bored," said Lulu.

I should have known enough to get scared right then. But I was too busy enjoying the parade, and worrying about what was going to happen next.

What happened next was that Myrna Smud showed up. Or, more accurately, we got to where Myrna and her crowd were waiting. They had gathered on the steps of city hall, where Myrna was making a speech.

"People of Syracuse!" she cried, "awake to the monsters in your midst!"

She was yelling through a megaphone. Her voice could be heard even above the music of our parade.

"Now I know why they call those things bull-horns," muttered Kevver.

The parade stopped. We were face to face with about a thousand people carrying signs that said, "BAM! BAM! Ban All Monsters!" and "Monsters Go Home!" and even "Frankenstein, Frankenstein. He is not a friend of mine."

"Monsters go home!" they shouted.

"That's right!" cried Myrna. "Save our children's imaginations. Drive these creatures from our midst!"

"Excuse me," said Lulu, squeezing past me. "I gotta go do something."

I was too worried about Myrna and the Bammers to realize that it was Lulu I should really be worrying about.

Suddenly the Count was standing next to the car. "I have never been so insulted in my life!" he declared. "I vill lodge a complaint with the Transylvanian Embassy first thing tomorrow morning."

"Does she mean us?" asked another voice. It was Goony. He was standing on the other side of the car. He was crying again.

"No more monsters! No more monsters!" chanted Myrna.

"No more monsters!" chanted the crowd on the steps.

Suddenly I heard another voice, also using a bullhorn. "Two bits, four bits, six bits, a dollar! If you love monsters, stand up and holler!"

It was Lulu! She had grabbed her father's megaphone, and was leading *our* crowd in a cheer. The people behind us began to shout and applaud.

"No more monsters!" cried Myrna.

"No more monsters!" shouted her followers.

"We love monsters!" screamed Lulu.

"We love monsters!" shouted our followers.

Then the voices all got kind of mixed up. "No More We Love Monsters Monsters Monsters!" screamed the mob.

Now Lulu was walking up the steps of City Hall. "Give me an *M*!"

"*M*!" roared the crowd.

"Give me an *O*!"

"*O*!" they screamed.

"*N-S-T-E-R*! Monster! Monster! *Monster*!"

The crowd went nuts—and so did Myrna. She hit Lulu over the head with her sign.

That was it—the battle was on. Most of the crowd didn't know that Lulu had spent her entire life doing things that made people want to hit her over the head. They only saw an overweight adult woman who should have known better bopping a little kid with a sign.

"Lulu!" cried Skip, racing up the steps of city hall.

"Lulu!" cried the crowd.

People were surging forward. Even the police lines couldn't hold them back. BAM! signs were going bam all around.

Then the moon slipped over the horizon. It looked huge behind the city towers.

I heard a horrible howl behind me. I turned and saw the Wolfman shaking and snarling as his big eyebrow seemed to spread over his entire face. His hands were getting hairy. His nails turned black, stretching out into sharp claws.

An instant later the Count vanished in a flash of smoke and a big black bat appeared in front of our car. Sigmund Fred was growling ominously. Quasimodo was leaping from car to car. The Mummy had started to moan. Steam was curling from Godzonga's mouth, and the little creature was bouncing up and down, waving its paws menacingly.

The monsters were basically nice guys. But if they got too excited I could see we would have a real problem on our hands.

What we needed was something to distract everyone.

I knew of one thing that might do the trick.

"Come on," I said to Kevver. "Time to bring out our surprise."

"I thought we were going to save it for the party," he protested.

"If we don't bring it out now, there might not be a party!" I said.

He nodded. We grabbed the keys out of the ignition. We climbed over the back of the car and opened the trunk. Inside was the package we had worked up with Wendy Moon over the last few weekends.

It took both of us to carry it. But we couldn't get anywhere. The crowd surging around us was too thick to make any progress. "Igor!" I cried. "Siggie! Give us a hand!"

Sigmund Fred came plowing through the crowd. Even in the grip of the riot, people cowered from the huge green monster. Igor was riding on Siggie's shoulders, shaking his fists and screaming at the people below.

Without even asking what we needed, Sigmund Fred stooped down and scooped up the device.

"Up on the steps!" I shouted in his ear.

He nodded and plunged back into the crowd. Kevver and I tried to follow, but we couldn't get anywhere. For a minute I thought everything was lost. Then the rest of the monsters appeared. They gathered around us in a V-formation, and plowed through the crowd after Sigmund Fred. Kevver and I were protected inside the wedge.

We got to the steps faster than I would have thought possible. Once we got onto the steps we were out of the worst of the riot. I looked back and shivered. I think I'd rather face a monster than a mob any day.

Sigmund put down the device. With the monsters clearing the way, Kevver went left and I went right. We stretched the device to its full length.

Then I pulled the trigger.

Familiar music began to blare. I turned it up. It still wasn't loud enough. I turned it up again.

People in the crowd began to notice that something new was happening. When they turned toward the music they saw it: a forty-eight foot long flag, rising from the steps of city hall.

What could they do?

With the speakers playing The Star Spangled Banner so loud you could hear it in the next county, everyone had to stop.

They all put their hands over their hearts and started to sing.

When you think about it, that's not a bad way to stop a riot.

Chapter Eighteen

The Monster of the Year

The police were not amused. So everyone who seemed to be involved in this mess—including me, Kevver, Myrna, Lulu, the monsters, and a half dozen of the top Bammers—was whisked off for questioning. The only one who escaped was the Count. He just flew away.

He headed straight for my house, which was how my mother knew what was going on even before we even had a chance to call her. She was not happy when she had to come to the police station to bail us out again.

The WERD party was going full swing when we finally arrived. Everyone seemed to be having a good time. Kevver and I were more nervous than ever. No matter who won, it seemed that we were going to be in trouble.

Then I got brilliant again. I guess desperation can do that for you. I whispered my idea to Kevver, and he nodded eagerly. We found Jeff and told him our plan. He agreed and even helped me write a little speech.

The contest began at midnight. Skip was the host. Kevver and I sat on the stage as a parade of monsters made their way past us, growling and snarling at the crowd. Our friends were all there, of course, as well as a lot of local people who had entered the contest just for the fun of it. Some of them had costumes so good I might have believed they were for real—if I hadn't already met the real thing.

Finally the parade was over. Kevver and I conferred for a few minutes. But that was just for show. We had already made up our minds.

We walked to the front of the stage.

"Have the judges made their decision?" asked Skip.

I nodded.

He handed me the microphone.

I looked out at that sea of masks and faces, a wonderful stew of monsters and humans. My hands began to tremble. I had never made a speech before.

Kevver was standing beside me, holding the prize. Siggie, the Count, and the other monsters were gathered on the stage behind me.

I tried to speak, but my throat seemed to have closed in on itself. I swallowed and tried again.

"Being the judge of the first Monster of the Year Contest was a great responsibility," I said. "We have been lucky enough to have some of the most popular monsters of all time participate. It has been a great privilege to meet and talk with these wonderful characters. We hope that they have enjoyed their stay in Syracuse as much as we have enjoyed having them."

I paused and everyone applauded politely.

The monsters smiled. But you could feel the nervous tension crackling between them. Who was going to be the winner?

I knew the answer, but I was still pretty tense. I had another question on my mind. Would I survive announcing the winner?

"Look at these great faces!" I cried, gesturing behind me.

The monsters all growled and snarled. People shrieked in appreciation.

I smiled. This was going better than I had expected. I realized that once you get over being nervous, talking to so many people is fun.

I held up my hands for silence.

"We want to thank these monsters for their participation. However, wonderful as they are, we all know that ugliness is only skin deep. So

the judges have decided that the first Monster of the Year prize should go to someone who has demonstrated what it really means to be a monster. Someone who wants to squeeze the human spirit, stifle imagination, and hold our hearts in bondage. Someone who wants to control what we think, what we see, what we hear, what we read. Someone who represents the tradition of the cruelest, most frightening monsters of all time—those who would bind not only our hands, but our hearts. Yes, ladies and gentlemen, the monster of the year is none other than— Myrna Smud!"

The crowd roared its approval.

I looked behind me nervously. At first the monsters looked confused.

Then they began to smile.

When the Count gave me a thumbs-up sign, I knew I was home free.

And that was about the end of it.

Oh, we still had some messy legal business to deal with. For a while it seemed like everyone was suing everyone. ("Lawyers!" cried the monsters. Then they all made that complicated hand gesture and spit through their finger *three* times.) But finally everyone agreed to drop charges against everyone else. It just seemed easier that way.

Actually, the monsters were gone by that time.

After all, as the count said, "Halloveen is almost here. Ve have vork to do!"

We do get an occasional letter from the gang. The publicity seems to have done them good. Some of them have been picking up extra money endorsing products and so on. They all seem happy.

Skip has kept in touch, too. I think he likes me and Kevver because we're almost normal.

One last thing. I should tell you that before the monsters left, they decided that getting together had been so much fun they wanted to have a convention every year.

So maybe you'd better keep a string of garlic in your kitchen just in case.

After all—next year they just might come to your town!

About the Author and Illustrator

Bruce Coville has written dozens of books for young readers, including, *My Teacher is an Alien, Sarah's Unicorn, The Monster's Ring,* and the Camp Haunted Hills books, *How I Survived My Summer Vacation* and *Some of My Best Friends Are Monsters.* He grew up in central New York, where he's lived most of his life. "My grandfather was a farmer, but also served as caretaker of the local cemetery and I spent a lot of time helping him there when I was growing up," he says. "Not only that, my school colors were orange and black. And my favorite holiday has always been Halloween. So sometimes I think I can't *help* writing monster stories." Before becoming a full-time writer, Bruce Coville worked as a magazine editor, a teacher, a toymaker, and a gravedigger.

Harvey Kurtzman invented *MAD* magazine, serving as editor for its first 28 issues. His art and humor have inspired comic book artists for over two decades, and have made millions of people laugh. He is also the author of *My Life as a Cartoonist*, available from Minstrel Books.